SEASIDE BONDS
LOBSTER BAY BOOK 5

MEREDITH SUMMERS

CHAPTER ONE

*L*iz Weston sat on the deck of Tides and looked out over the sugar sand beach at the glistening ocean waves. She was glad she'd decided to splurge on accommodations at the old inn located in her hometown of Lobster Bay, Maine. The rooms were cozy, the service impeccable, and the view gorgeous.

The crashing of the waves, the tang of the salty sea air, and the gulls darting above created a peaceful atmosphere. She wrapped her sweater around her to ward off the slight Maine chill. Summer had passed. Now it was early fall, which, in her opinion, was the best time to be at the beach, since it wasn't crowded with tourists.

But she wasn't back in her hometown to visit the beach. She was here to clean out her old family home. For most people, a visit to their hometown would be a fun trip, but not to Liz. Her childhood memories weren't exactly pleasant.

She'd volunteered to do this job because she was always the one who did the dirty work in her family. Always the one everyone else depended on. But that wasn't the only reason. The inn was a distraction from her own problems, not to mention a nice place to stay—something she currently didn't have.

"I never get tired of this view." Jane Miller, proprietor of Tides, stood beside her holding a coffee pot. The proprietor's golden retriever, Cooper, waited obediently at her side. Jane gestured towards Liz's empty mug, and Liz slid it over for a top-off.

Liz was a few years younger than Jane, so they hadn't known each other well in school. Of course, all the families in a town as small as Lobster Bay knew one another, and Liz knew Jane's family had owned the inn for generations.

"It must be wonderful living right here on the beach." Liz's childhood home was several blocks from the beach. No ocean view or sound of waves, but she could walk to the beach in twenty minutes. That had been her escape when her father started yelling.

She glanced up at Jane, who was gazing blissfully out at the ocean. Liz was forty-five, and she guessed Jane must be almost fifty. She looked younger, though. Jane was tall and thin, and her silver hair looked sassy in a trendy short haircut, while her blue eyes sparkled with life. She looked happy, at peace. A woman comfortable in her own skin.

Had Liz ever felt that way about herself? The last few

years had been hard. First Kyle leaving her for a younger woman, then Dad getting sick and Liz having to deal with her feelings for her father and argue with siblings to manage his care. All that was over now, but she still felt a bit beaten down. Maybe a trendy haircut like Jane's and a new health regimen would help.

"It is. But there was a time when I thought we might lose this property." Jane's words pulled Liz out of her thoughts.

"Really? But your family has owned it for generations."

"Yeah. My mom started having memory issues, and we didn't realize what was going on until she'd almost run the business into the ground." Jane sighed. "I set aside my retirement plans to help straighten things out, and here I am."

"Memory problems? I remember your mom. She was a real dynamo."

"Still is. I'm sorry about your dad. He was at Tall Pines, same as Mom. I remember talking to him a few times at movie night." Jane said. "Nice guy."

Liz simply smiled and said thanks. In truth, her father really wasn't a nice guy. Or at least he hadn't been when she was growing up. Gruff, strict, always yelling and belittling her.

Liz reached out and ruffled Cooper's fur. "It's so great that you have a dog here. I love dogs, but it's been a while since I've had one. My husband wasn't that keen on them."

Memories of Major, the German shepherd they'd had when they'd first been married, bubbled up. Liz had adored that dog. Back then, Kyle had been nicer to her. But after Major had passed, he'd forbidden her to get another dog. She should have stood up to him and insisted on it, but it hadn't seemed worth the fight at the time. One good thing about him leaving was that now she could do whatever she wanted.

"Guests seem to like Cooper. At first, I thought he might be off-putting, but it turns out he's quite an attraction."

"No doubt."

"Are you staying in town long?"

"Long as it takes to clean up the house and put it up for sale."

"Oh, your dad still had the house here in town?"

"My siblings and I couldn't agree on whether to sell it or not after he had the stroke. My brother and sister always thought maybe Dad would come back home." Liz sighed. "But he never did, and the house has been sitting empty for over almost six years now. Right now, there's no electricity, even, and it's kind of a mess, which is why I'm staying here." Liz glanced out at the ocean. "Plus, the view is better."

"Oh, gosh, well, I hope things go well at your dad's. Do you need anything else? More coffee?" Jane asked.

Liz shook her head. Two cups were enough for her. "No thank you. I'd better get in gear and start on the house."

"Okay. Have a great day."

"You too." Liz watched Jane and Cooper leave, thinking wistfully of how happy Jane seemed.

Liz wished she could be that happy, but right now, she was on a bit of a downswing. Things weren't exactly turning out the way she'd planned. Not only did cleaning out the family home mean revisiting unwanted childhood memories, it also reminded her that she had no place to live. The small apartment she'd rented after the divorce was being turned into condos, and she couldn't afford one because she had limited savings and was too young to tap into her retirement money.

It had been a mistake to take early retirement from her position at the school, but how was she to know that her husband would spend their life savings and leave her with no house and very little money? At least she would get something from the sale of her father's house. But first, she needed to clean it out and spruce it up so someone would actually want to buy it.

She took one last look at the ocean and then pushed back from the table. She dreaded going to that house, but she couldn't really put it off any longer.

CHAPTER TWO

*J*ane hung her white apron on the hook in the kitchen and clipped the leash to Cooper's collar. She didn't remember Liz well from when they were kids, but she had empathy for the woman. Liz seemed a little bit sad and lost, and Jane felt bad that Liz apparently hadn't gotten along with her father.

Having had a wonderful relationship with both of her parents, Jane couldn't imagine what a bad one would be like. She hoped that while Liz was in town, she could make peace with the past.

It was funny because Mr. Weston had always seemed nice whenever she'd interacted with him at Tall Pines, the assisted living facility where Jane's mom, Addie, lived. He'd always been ready with a warm smile, never bitter and angry like some of the people that lived there. It was hard to imagine him not being a good father, but people often mellowed as they aged.

Brenda, the cook, was just cleaning up the breakfast dishes.

"I'm off to Sandcastles. You're in charge." Jane met her sister and best friends for coffee several mornings a week at Sandcastles Bakery, which was owned by one of her friends, Claire.

Brenda hung the dish drying towel over the faucet. "Okee-doke. I can hold down the fort until Andie comes in an hour."

"Thank you." Jane gave her a little hug. She didn't know what she would do without Brenda. She'd been working at Tides as long as Jane could remember and had helped her mother immensely, especially when Addie's memory had started to fail.

Jane's phone dinged as she rushed out the door. She smiled when she saw a text from her boyfriend, Mike. But the smile faded when she noticed the text's subject.

How is the search for a helper going?

Jane had met Mike earlier that summer, and the two became fast friends and then even more. These days, she spent a lot of time at Mike's new condo, but she still had a lot of responsibilities at Tides. Mike had been urging her to find some good help so she could take more time off. And she deserved time off. After all, she was supposed to be retired now but had delayed her retirement to run the place after her mother got sick.

But it was hard to find someone to run things. It had to be someone she trusted with her family business. Someone who would show up on time. Someone who would be pleasant and cordial to the guests. In a small town like Lobster Bay, that special someone was hard to find.

Working on it!

She felt guilty as she typed the response because she wasn't exactly *working* on it—more like thinking about it.

"Who are we going to get to help at the inn?" she asked Cooper as they walked the two blocks through the quaint town to the bakery.

Cooper glanced up at her. Was he frowning? It certainly seemed that way. Perhaps he was criticizing her lack of effort on the subject.

"I know I should be looking harder. Should I put an ad in the paper?"

Cooper answered her by stopping to sniff a shrub on the corner.

"But I love running the inn now and greeting the guests myself…"

Cooper barked softly.

"I know it's not fair to expect Andie to keep coming over to watch the place. She has her own business."

When their mom's memory issues had boiled over, Andie came back to town just to help for a little while. It was a bit awkward because the two sisters hadn't been especially close as adults. Andie had left town decades ago for an important job in the big city and rarely came to visit. But she'd decided to stay, and Jane was pleased their relationship had been rekindled. Now Andie had a thriving antique business in town, and she deserved to spend most of her time on that.

Sandcastles, with its multihued awning and sidewalk café, came into view, and Jane picked up the pace. She could see her friends Maxi and Claire seated at a round table near the large planter, which was brimming with colorful flowers even this late in the season. Andie wasn't there yet, but a plate of pastries was already on the table, and steam swirled up from the coffee mugs at each place setting.

She made a mental note to work harder to find someone who would take some shifts at Tides. She and Mike were going to meet that night for dinner at one of their favorite restaurants, Oarweeds, and she wanted to have some progress to report to him.

"Maybe it will be nice enough to sit out on the patio for dinner tonight," she said to Cooper.

Cooper wagged his tail.

"And hopefully I'll be able to talk about a better plan for getting help at Tides so Mike won't be disappointed."

CHAPTER THREE

*A*ndie Miller crept down the back stairs from her second-floor apartment to her antique shop. She still couldn't believe the shop was all hers.

She loved the scent of old wood and furniture polish, the soft ticking of the grandfather clock, and the creak of the hardwood floors softened by the Oriental rugs on top of them. Why had she resisted coming home to Lobster Bay for so long?

Once, she'd thought being an appraiser for Christie's in New York was the best career. She'd wanted to grab that big once-in-a-lifetime antique find. Lobster Bay had seemed like a step backward.

But now, she felt differently. Good riddance to her old job in the noisy, smog-filled city. The fresh ocean air and simple small-town life suited her much better. And the excitement of finding new treasures with local estate sales and helping the people in her town get money for their antiques was a lot better than searching for a big find that never came.

Little everyday discoveries were much more fun. Like the ones she'd been finding in the estates she'd recently acquired. One estate had been loaded with antique furniture, high-boy servers decorated with ornate carvings, sterling silver tea sets, and hand-painted porcelain. The other, smaller estate had several boxes of hand-embroidered linens, silver place settings, and some vanity items like perfume bottles and ivory brushes. She hadn't even had a chance to go through all the boxes yet.

It was Tuesday, so Andie was meeting her sister and their friends at Sandcastles in an hour for their morning coffee and pastry. She didn't want to miss that. It was her favorite time of the week. But she was an early riser who kept her window shades open to see the sun coming up over the ocean every morning, and since she'd been up too early to meet at Sandcastles, she couldn't resist looking through one of the boxes from the estate.

After setting aside the decades-old yellow newspaper, she pulled out an emerald glass glove box with yellow and white enamel flowers painted on it. She was surprised to find it had no chips or cracks. Someone had taken good care of it.

Next, she picked up an old humidor with ivory inlay. A few little pieces of ivory were missing, but that was normal for this type of item. A collector would still want it, since it was an unusual piece and in good enough condition.

Some old scraps of clothing lay underneath the humidor and a trio of brass buttons. On the bottom was an old black cylinder. Was something inside?

The cylinder didn't seem as old as the other things in the box. Perhaps someone had rolled up a rare painting at a later date? A trill of excitement ran through her as she popped the end off and peered inside to see the brittle edges of a piece of yellowed paper. She took it to the counter, carefully pried the paper out, then unrolled it. Civil War discharge papers!

Apparently, Robert P. Koslachowski had served in the Civil War and been honorably discharged. It was an exciting find but not something Andie would ever think about selling. This item belonged with Robert Koslachowski's descendants. She'd bought the items from someone named Nadine Parker, so Koslachowski must have been her ancestor. She'd get in touch with Nadine so she could come and pick up the discharge papers and the old buttons and scraps of fabric, which must have been what was left of Robert's uniform.

She could call Nadine while she was taking her shift at Tides. She was happy to help out at the family inn, even if it did take her away from her antique business a bit. She hated that Jane was tied to the place and wanted to give her a break whenever she could. But Jane had mentioned hiring someone else to take some shifts, and Andie, for one, would be pretty happy if that happened.

Movement across the street caught her eye. She looked over at the hair salon, Curlz, where the proprietor,

Mary, was opening up. The two women waved at each other. Andie and Mary had formed a bond in the time she'd been in Lobster Bay, a bond made even stronger because Andie was dating Mary's nephew, Shane.

Shoot! She was late for her meeting at Sandcastles! She carefully stored the Civil War papers in a drawer then swiped the dust from her T-shirt and headed out the front door.

CHAPTER FOUR

The outdoor seating at Sandcastles was full, just as it was every morning, despite the slight chill in the morning air. Hailey was topping off coffee mugs. Maxi was mostly content sitting there with her best friends since childhood, Claire and Jane, and waiting for Andie to arrive. She pinched a piece off her bran muffin and slipped it under the table to Cooper, who was sitting obediently at Jane's feet.

Cooper looked up at her with adoring eyes, and she tried to analyze the look in them for the pet portrait she had been commissioned to paint. Was it the highlights that made them so expressive? The depth of color? The shading?

She was worried about the pet portrait. She'd finished many paintings before, but those were landscapes. She'd never painted animals, and this commission was important because it was to commemorate Sandcastles regulars Bert and Harry's pug, Goblin, who had recently passed away.

She bent down to get a closer look at Cooper, pushing silvery-blond curls out of her face as she studied the dog.

"Did you drop something?" Claire asked from the other side of the table.

Maxi looked up at her friend, who was tucking a strand of her wavy auburn hair into a clip, a questioning look in her golden-flecked hazel eyes. "No, just studying Cooper for my commission. I'm a little nervous about getting it right."

"You're having a hard time with it?" Jane asked.

"Unfortunately, yes."

"Don't worry, you're a great artist. You'll nail it," Jane reassured her.

But Maxi *was* worried. "I just want to capture Goblin's essence and show her heart so when Bert and Harry look at the painting, they can feel the joy they had with Goblin and not be sad that she isn't around anymore."

"That's sweet." Claire put her hand on Maxi's arm. "I'm sure you'll pull it off."

"What's sweet?" Andie appeared at the table, frowning at Claire. The expression in Andie's hazel eyes indicated she didn't like anything sweet or mushy. Today, she was wearing her long dark hair in a messy bun on top of her head and had on a plain T-shirt and jeans that apparently had some dust on the side. Knowing Andie, she'd probably just come from rooting around in an attic for antiques.

Jane scooted over to make room as Hailey set a mug in front of Andie and poured some coffee into it.

"Maxi's doing a painting of Goblin for Bert and Harry," Claire said.

Andie's face softened. "Awww, that is nice."

"So, anyway, how are things going with you guys?" Maxi changed the subject. She was uncomfortable talking about herself and didn't want to bring everyone down with her problems. She gestured to the papers on the table in front of Claire. "What's all this?"

"I'm trying to come up with some new recipes for fall. Pumpkin muffins, spiced coffees, that sort of thing. Rob is doing the same at his place. He's been baking tons of pumpkin bread."

They all looked across the street to Bradford Breads, where Rob was putting out a sign with the latest sale items. He glanced over and waved.

Claire blushed. Once, the two had been competitors. Now, they were an item. They were deliriously happy together, which pleased Maxi. It was funny to think that at one time Claire thought Sandcastles would be threatened by the new bread store Rob had opened across the street.

"I ordered some of his pumpkin breads for Tides," Jane said.

"How is business with the summer winding down?" Maxi asked.

"Slowing down a bit, but I'm going to do some fall

specials to bring people in. Getaway weekends, apple cider tastings, that sort of thing." Jane slathered butter on half of her blueberry muffin. She had two chocolate chip muffins in a bag for her mother, Addie. Claire always sent a few of Addie's favorite muffins when Jane went to visit her mother at Tall Pines. "Liz Weston is back in town and staying at Tides while she cleans out her family home. You guys remember her?"

Andie frowned. "I think I remember her brother. Peter?"

Claire shook her head. "The last name is familiar, but I don't think I knew any of them."

"I remember them vaguely," Maxi said. "Their dad was kind of mean, wasn't he?"

Jane looked up from her muffin. "Liz alluded to that as well, but I met him a few times at Tall Pines, and he was very nice."

Max shrugged. "People change."

Jane nodded. "Anyway, she's the only guest right now, but we have a few other reservations. It's pretty slow overall, though, and as I recall, this is the slowest time with kids going back to school and no one going on vacation. Which is a good thing since I can't seem to find anyone to work there."

"No luck in the search?" Claire looked up from the paperwork. "Maybe Hailey knows someone."

"Hailey knows someone who for what?" Hailey appeared at their table with her endless coffee pot.

"To work part-time at Tides."

Hailey pressed her lips together. "You know I really don't know anyone looking for that kind of work. Most of my friends have full-time jobs."

"You're looking to hire someone for a part-time job?" Sally Littlefield, the town handywoman, who had been fixing one of the large planters that separated the outdoor café area from the sidewalk, peeked at them over the purple petunias that spilled out of the planter. Her bright blue eyes assessed Jane from underneath silver bangs, and Jane nodded.

Of course, Jane should've realized that if anyone knew someone in town who was looking for this kind of work, it would be Sally. She'd lived in town for most of her seventy-odd years and knew everyone. "Just to fill in part-time. I still want to work there, but Mike wants me to spend less time at work, and Andie has her antique business."

Sally screwed up her tanned, weathered face. She pushed the long silver braid back over her shoulder. "You know I can't think of anyone offhand, but I'll ask around."

"Thanks." Jane settled back in her seat. "I guess I can check the task of looking for an employee off my list now."

Everyone laughed.

"So, what's going on with you, Andie?" Claire asked.

"Nothing much. And I don't mind helping out at Tides, Jane. I could do more hours."

Jane stole a piece of corn muffin from Andie's plate.

"I know. But you have your business to run. We can afford to hire someone part-time, and we should."

"That would give me more time to process estates like the one that just came in. Do you guys know a family by the last name of Koslachowski?"

Everyone looked around and shook their heads.

"No. I think I'd remember that name," Claire said.

"Someone came in and sold me several dusty old boxes from their attic. I found some Civil War discharge papers and part of a uniform in one of the boxes. I figured the family would want the papers and uniform back, but I've never heard of them. Must be some long-forgotten relative of the woman who sold me the box."

That seemed like an easy problem to solve, Maxi thought as she sat back and nibbled on her muffin. If only all problems were as easy. Her thoughts drifted to the painting. How could she figure out how to give the painting that real feeling of warmth and love one experienced when they looked into the eyes of their pet?

CHAPTER FIVE

"The house is in a lot worse shape than I thought." Liz stood in the avocado and gold kitchen of her childhood home, talking on the phone to her sister, Shelly.

She hadn't been inside the house in over ten years. Now it was clear her father had struggled in the years after her mother's death. When her father had become ill, her brother was the one to close up the house. He'd never mentioned the items piled on the counters, the clutter in every room, and the layers of dust. Her mother, who had died years before, would be appalled at the condition.

Sudden guilt washed over her. Should she have come back to help her father in those years after her mother's death? She'd returned to visit a few times but never for long, always opting to meet her father somewhere for a quick lunch. When he'd gone into assisted living at Tall

Pines, she'd visited once a year but never returned to the house.

"Does it still have that orange and brown shag carpet that Mom wanted to get rid of years ago?" Shelly asked.

"Yep." The carpet, which was once fluffy and colorful, was now matted and dull. "Looks like Dad hasn't vacuumed it since she died."

"Well, the house has been empty for almost six years. It's sure to be showing some signs of age and neglect."

"Yeah, there is lots of dust… and spiders." Liz shuddered as one ran across the wall to a web in the corner.

"I just wish Dad had a chance to go back home after the stroke. That was all he really wanted." Shelly sounded teary-eyed.

Liz sighed. She'd argued with Shelly and her brother, Peter, about keeping the house. They never gave up hope that their father would come home.

"Thanks for doing all of this with the house," Shelly was saying. "I'm so busy at work I can't break away right now."

Just because Liz had taken early retirement, her siblings thought she had nothing better to do while they were still too busy with their jobs. They were partly right. She didn't have much else to do and nowhere else to go, not that they knew about that.

Maybe she was being too hard on them. After all, she had volunteered, and they did have jobs. They'd both come for the funeral, of course, and offered to help, but Liz had brushed them off. It was her own fault.

"It's okay. I don't mind," Liz said.

"You sure?"

"Yep."

"How is the yard?" Shelly asked. "We were paying someone to tend to it. I hope they did a good job."

Liz stepped over a pile of boxes on her way to the big picture window in the living room. Someone—either Peter or her father—had closed the drapes the last time they'd been here, and now it was dark as a cave.

She pulled the thick drapes back. Sun streamed in, highlighting the particles of dust released from the drapes like a snow globe.

The gorgeous maple tree they'd climbed as kids was still in the front yard. She almost smiled as she remembered how pretty it was with its bright-red leaves later in the fall. But then raking the leaves…

"It looks fine." The grass was a little yellow but freshly mowed, and the shrubs were neatly trimmed. The yard could use some of the flowers that her mother used to plant to add some color, but that would be for the new owners to worry about.

"Is it really bad? The fees at Tall Pines took most of Dad's money, but I suppose we could scrape some together for repairs," Shelly said.

Liz hoped the "we" didn't include her. She had nothing to scrape together. But Shelly didn't need to know that. "I think it just needs a good cleaning."

She wandered into the bathroom, which had pink tile and a matching toilet from the 1960s. Her mother had pestered her father to upgrade it in the '80s, but they'd never gotten around to it. "It is a bit outdated, though."

"Maybe we could spruce it up?"

"We?"

Shelly paused. "I could see if I can get time off, but we have a big event coming up and…"

"No, don't worry. I'll see what I can do. I'll check with some realtors and see what they think. Maybe people want houses with vintage charm."

She wandered back to the kitchen and saw a woman standing at the fence and craning her neck toward the house. She looked to be a hundred if she was a day. When Liz and her siblings were kids, the O'Donnells had lived in that house, but that couldn't possibly be Mrs. O'Donnell, could it?

As she watched, the woman crossed her arms over her chest, made a beeline down the length of the fence, and then proceeded into her yard and toward the front door.

"Shell? I gotta go. Looks like I'm about to get a visitor." Liz hung up and hurried to the front door.

"Can I help you?" Liz peered down at the woman, who was studying her with suspicion.

"I think the question is can I help *you*?" The woman waved toward the house. "Last I heard, this is Frank Weston's house."

"Oh! Sorry." Liz stuck out her hand. "I'm his daughter, Liz."

"Oh." The woman shook her hand. "Bunny Howard."

"Howard. What happened to the O'Donnells?"

"Ted and I bought the house from them fifteen years ago. I've been picking your father's tomatoes."

Huh? Liz glanced out toward the backyard, where the garden used to be when she was little. It looked a bit overgrown. "He still had a garden?"

"Yep."

"But it's been six years since he's been here. Surely nothing would still be growing through all those winters."

Bunny shrugged. "I thought he might get better, so I planted, fertilized, and harvested. Do you want some? I have the last of them ripening on the kitchen window."

"Umm... no thanks." The thought of biting into a sweet, juicy garden tomato did make her mouth water, though.

"I was sorry to hear of your father's passing. He was one of the good ones."

"He was?" Liz wondered if maybe Bunny had the wrong house. Then again, maybe she had known her father in a different capacity, and Liz supposed it was possible he had mellowed. To be honest, her father hadn't seemed quite as mean when she'd visited him at Tall Pines, but her unpleasant memories had always colored those visits.

"Oh yeah. After Ted passed your dad helped me fix the back shed, put up Christmas lights, even shoveled my driveway. He played a mean game of poker too."

"You played poker with my father?" Liz couldn't picture her father playing poker. Maybe she hadn't known him as well as she'd thought.

"Sure!" Bunny smiled at the memory, then her eyes narrowed. "Not that strip kind you young folks play. Regular poker. He was a friend. That's all, no hanky-panky."

Liz almost laughed picturing her dad playing strip poker and engaging in hanky-panky. "Are you sure you're talking about Frank Weston?"

"Yes, of course. You said you were his daughter, didn't you?" Bunny looked confused.

"I am. I just can't picture him playing poker. Did you know Mom?"

Bunny smiled again. "A little bit. She was a lovely woman. So sad that she died so young and left your father a widower. He was very lonely. Such a nice guy." Bunny looked at her as if wondering why she hadn't come to visit more often.

"My siblings and I live far away."

"Of course. Well, I just wanted to make sure you had permission to be here."

"I'll be here every day." Liz gestured to the mess in the house behind her. "Need to clean the place out and get it up for sale."

"For sale? Your dad always hoped one of his kids would move here."

Why? The house wasn't exactly a grand estate that had been in the family for generations. "Umm, I don't think so."

Bunny simply smiled and then turned to go. "Okay,

dear, let me know if you need any help. I'm right next door."

"Great, thanks."

Bunny left, and Liz turned back to the house. It looked like a time capsule from a hoarder. Where in the world would she start?

CHAPTER SIX

When Andie arrived at Tides for her shift, she found Brenda sitting behind the check-in desk in the foyer and a large tray of freshly baked chocolate chip cookies on the side table. Andie grabbed a cookie as she walked past.

"Those are for the guests!" Brenda admonished.

Andie turned around to survey the empty lobby as she took a bite. "What guests?"

"Very funny. It's still nice out, and someone driving up the coast could decide they want a room."

Andie eyed the three dozen cookies in the tray. They didn't even have that many rooms. "That would be great if they do. I promise I won't eat any more."

Brenda laughed. "At least rearrange the tray so there isn't an empty spot."

"I will, and now that I'm here, you can head out."

"Are you sure? You have a business to run. I can stay a little later."

Andie was sure. She didn't mind taking shifts at Tides. She loved it here. Everything from her great-grandfather's old writing desk to her grandmother's flow blue china to the antique paintings that had hung on the wall was familiar and comforting. "I don't mind watching the place. Don't you have some grandkids' soccer games to attend or something?"

Brenda's eyes lit up at the mention of her grandkids. She doted on them. "Well, if you're sure…"

"I am."

Brenda grabbed her purse from under the counter, and Andie had a thought. Brenda's family had been in town for ages, and even though she was only about twenty years older than Andie, she might be able to help find the family those Civil War papers belonged to.

"Hey, Brenda, do you know a family with the last name Koslachowski?"

Brenda pressed her lips together and tilted her head as she repeated the name. "Can't say I do. Why?"

Andie told her about the Civil War papers. "I just want to return them to the family. I'm sure the person I bought them from is a distant relative, but I was just curious because I didn't recognize the name."

"Well, I'm sure you'll get them into the right hands."

They said their good-byes, and Brenda left.

Andie looked up Nadine Parker in her contacts and

was about to call her when Liz Weston, covered in dust and sneezing, came breezing into the lobby.

Liz looked up to see Andie. "Oh, hello. Where's Jane?"

"She's off this afternoon. I'm her sister, Andie." From the way Liz had strolled in, Andie figured she was staying there, and they only had one guest right now, so it wasn't hard to figure out who the woman was. "Are you Liz Weston?"

Liz looked down at her outfit. "How did you guess? Did Jane tell you I was going to clean out a house that has been closed up for six years?"

Andie laughed. "It's kinda obvious, plus you're our only guest."

Liz smiled, but she seemed a little down in the dumps.

"It's hard going through all your family memories, isn't it?" Andie asked.

"You sound like you know what you're talking about."

Andie glanced around the lobby. "Well, not personally. All our family memories are here. My parents and sister and I didn't live at the inn, but my grandparents did, and we always spent a lot of time here. But I used to be an appraiser at Christie's, and many of my clients were clearing out old family estates, and I know there are a lot of memories that bubble up. You should take your time and be kind to yourself."

Liz looked about to burst into tears, so Andie rushed over to the cookie tray. "Cookie? Brenda made them from scratch earlier today."

That got a smile. Liz took a cookie. "You know, it is hard. I haven't been back to the house in a long time, and Dad has been in Tall Pines for six years. There's a lot of dust, and I guess before that, he wasn't that great of a housekeeper."

"Are you selling it?" Andie asked.

Liz nodded. "I own it with my sister and brother now, and none of us live in town, so that's the best thing to do."

"Where do you live?" Andie asked.

Liz hesitated. "Well, I'm actually in a bit of a transition. I spent the last twenty years in Vermont, and I've had a bit of upheaval in my life lately, not the least of which was Dad's illness."

Andie nodded sympathetically while Liz munched on her cookie and glanced out through the sitting room to the ocean beyond. "Though I have to say Vermont has pretty mountains, but nothing beats the ocean."

"You just inherited a house right near the ocean. Maybe selling isn't the right thing?" Andie sensed that Liz needed some direction. She didn't know what kind of upheaval she'd had, but Andie could sympathize, since she'd gone through an upheaval herself just that past year.

"You know, living in Lobster Bay wouldn't be too bad but not in that house. That's the house I grew up in. It's outdated and looks like something from *That '70s Show*. I could never live there even if I could afford to buy out my siblings."

"You said the house is full of stuff? The mid-century era is really popular with collectors right now, and there might be some good antiques in there. If you want, I could take a look and let you know if anything's valuable. I'd hate for you to throw out something that was a desirable collectable." Andie was always on the lookout for old treasures and figured doing that could help Liz. "You'd be surprised at some of the things that are valuable. Vases that you think are junk, outdated furniture, even old kitchenware."

Liz grabbed another cookie and headed toward the stairs. "You know, I just might take you up on that."

Andie called Nadine Parker and explained the Civil War papers.

"Well, I'm afraid I can't help you there. We bought the house recently as a fixer-upper, and I found those boxes in the attic. I have no idea who that family is."

"Could you tell me who you bought it from? I could trace the family back through that."

"Actually, we got it at a bank auction because it had been foreclosed on. I don't know who owned it before us. Maybe the bank would help you out?"

Andie had a sinking feeling as she hung up the phone. Would the bank disclose that information? And if they wouldn't, how could she know who to return the Civil War items to?

CHAPTER SEVEN

Maxi stood in the Lobster Bay art gallery admiring the new display of impressionist paintings hanging on the wall. They showed ocean scenes by a Kennebunk, Maine, artist who was known for his use of wide brush strokes with bold colors and masterful contrast of light and dark.

The art gallery was one of her favorite places and where she came when she was feeling a bit off. The main room was always quiet and peaceful. The white walls were a perfect backdrop to showcase the paintings and sculptures. A few strategically located potted plants softened the area and brought nature inside. The light streaming in from the two-story windows bathed the paintings in a golden glow, especially in the late afternoon, when it slanted in at an angle, as it was doing right now.

"Beautiful, aren't they?" Muriel Fox, who worked at

the gallery a few days a week, looked chipper this morning. She had short cropped white hair that framed a tanned face. Her turquoise blouse and rainbow-striped broomstick skirt added color. Dozens of bangles jangled on her wrist as she crossed her arms over her chest and stood back to admire the painting.

"Gorgeous. I love the use of color and how the sunlight dances on top of the waves."

"Me too." Muriel turned from the painting. "So, what brings you in? Just admiring art today or another reason?"

Maxi sighed. "I have a bit of a problem, and it usually helps me to come here and think."

Muriel looked concerned. "Nothing too serious, I hope."

Muriel had been instrumental in helping Maxi reconnect with her love of painting. If anyone could help, she could. Maxi told her about the commission to paint Goblin and how important it was for her to get it right.

"So what's the problem? Perspective? Color? Fur techniques? Animals are much different than landscapes," Muriel said.

"You can say that again. I think the problem is that I can't capture the embodiment of Goblin's character. The life in her eyes. The expression on her face."

"Ahh, yes, makes sense. Have you tried practicing on something that isn't so important? The anxiety of getting it right might be blocking your creativity. I know how Bert and Harry loved her. She was such a good dog."

Muriel might be on to something. Maybe Maxi had

been trying too hard. Putting too much weight on getting it perfect. "That's good advice. I went right into painting Goblin, and it does feel a bit stressful. Maybe I will practice on my cats, Rembrandt and Picasso. I can relax when there's not so much riding on the outcome." Just thinking about her two cats—one solid white and one solid black—made Maxi smile. She'd gotten them as kittens over the summer, and while they'd grown a lot, they weren't full-grown yet and still got into everything.

Suddenly more optimistic, Maxi hitched her blue-and-white-striped tote bag up on her shoulder. "Thanks, Muriel. As usual, you have great advice."

"If that doesn't work, you might consider a lesson. I know someone right in town who is a master at animals. Let me write down her number." Muriel grabbed a business card from the desk and scribbled something on the back. "Her name is Bunny Howard. She's getting on in years, but I think she'll be happy to help you out."

Maxi took the card and rushed out. She was suddenly eager to get to the little cottage on the beach that she used as an art studio.

It was a short walk to her car in Perkins Cove, and the fresh air felt great. She spotted Jane and Mike heading into Oarweeds, but she didn't have time to visit with them. She needed to get to her cottage while there was still some natural light for her to paint by.

CHAPTER EIGHT

Jane felt lucky to have snagged an early dinner reservation at Oarweeds. The day still had some natural light by which to see the ocean from their patio table that overlooked the small cove.

She'd called ahead for an outdoor table so she could bring Cooper. He was now lying in between her and Mike, contentedly watching the people passing by as they walked along a popular path called the Marginal Way, which wound along the cliffs next to the ocean. There was a lot of foot traffic because it was the perfect early fall night for walking.

"I never get tired of dining outside." Jane dipped a piece of bread into the puddle of olive oil and balsamic vinegar she'd poured onto her small appetizer plate.

"Me too. You can't beat the view." Mike gazed out at the ocean.

"You can say that again." Jane let out a sigh of contentment. With Cooper and Mike at her side, the salty ocean air, sounds of the waves rushing over the rocky cove, and a lobster roll on the way, what could be better?

Mike turned to her and put his hand over hers. "I don't want to be a pest, but have you made any headway getting someone to help you out at Tides? You know if you got more help at the inn, we could do this more often."

Way to bring the mood down. Jane knew he meant well and wasn't doing it in a nagging way. He only wanted what was best. Any girl should be flattered that Mike wanted to spend more time with her. When she looked across the table into his green eyes, she saw only concern for her.

Jane looked away, pretending to adjust the napkin in her lap.

"I've got some feelers out." It wasn't exactly a lie. She'd asked around at Sandcastles just that morning. But she had to admit she could do more.

"That's my girl. I know it's hard to trust it to someone else, but you and Andie deserve to have free time to do your own thing."

"You're right. I can get so caught up with what's going on at the inn, and I really need to let go."

The waitress came to their table, bearing Jane's lobster roll in a grilled bun and Mike's clam chowder and broiled scallops. The pair ate in companionable silence for the first few bites.

"How was your day?" Mike asked as he dropped a few more oyster crackers into his chowder.

"Pretty slow. We only have one guest, Liz Weston. She grew up here in town and is back clearing out her father's house."

"Did you grow up with her?" Mike was from Seattle, so he wouldn't have known Liz, but he knew that Jane was familiar with practically every family in town.

"Not well, but her dad was at Tall Pines with Mom." Jane picked a piece of lobster out of the roll with her fork. They always stuffed them so full of meat it was hard to get a bite without taking some out. "He seemed nice."

"How is Addie? Did you visit her today?"

"She's great. She was painting another one of her watercolors when I visited today. I can't believe I resisted putting her in Tall Pines for so long. That place has been great for her." It had been heartbreaking for Jane to put her mother in an assisted living place, but Jane couldn't care for Addie herself. That decision turned out to be a blessing. Addie was getting much better care there, and Jane was free to run the family inn and live her life.

"Did you take Cooper?" Mike flipped Cooper an oyster cracker.

"Yes, everyone loves to see him so much." Cooper was always welcome at Tall Pines and seemed to put everyone in a good mood.

"Next time, give me a shout, and if I don't have any meetings, I'll go with you. I love visiting Addie too."

"She loves seeing you too." Jane's heart warmed.

Mike was a nice guy—successful, handsome, and he loved her mother. What more could she ask for? He never asked for anything except to spend more time with her. She was crazy not to make searching for another person to help out at Tides her top priority.

But a part of her wondered if she was hesitating for a self-destructive reason. After her husband had died, she'd distanced herself from any romantic entanglements. Until Mike. But now she had to wonder if maybe she just wasn't meant to be with anyone else.

They settled into small talk about things going on in the town, Mike's job, and their various friends. Over the summer they'd settled into a comfortable routine of hanging around with her best friends and their significant others. She loved spending time with Maxi and James, Claire and Rob, and Andie and Shane.

Things were going very well for her. She made a mental note to step up her search for the perfect person for Tides, since she didn't want to mess things up with Mike. And if her subconscious was trying to meddle, it would just have to butt out.

CHAPTER NINE

The next morning, Liz lingered over coffee on Tides's back deck before leaving for her dad's house. Funny, she still thought of it as her father's house instead of her home, even though she grew up there.

"How did things go at your house? Still no electricity?" Jane asked.

"It's getting turned on today, but the place is such a mess. I don't think I'll stay there even when the lights get turned on." Liz had been surprised that spending time in the house was less horrible than as she'd expected. She still had no desire to sleep there, though. "I met a neighbor, Bunny Howard. She seemed nice. Apparently, she's been keeping my father's garden up all these years. Isn't that odd?"

"I'm sorry, what?"

Jane had been staring out at the ocean, apparently lost in her own thoughts. She looked troubled. Liz's instincts as a school guidance counselor took over. Maybe it would help if she talked to someone and took a break from her own troubles. "Are you okay?"

"Oh, it's nothing really. How could I not be okay with this great view?" Jane topped off her coffee. "Did you ask me a question?"

Apparently, Jane wasn't ready to open up, so Liz continued talking about the house. "It was nothing. Straightening out that house is a bit overwhelming. I don't think Dad ever threw anything out. I met your sister in the lobby yesterday, and she said she'd take a look to see if anything was valuable."

"That's great. If there's anything of value, Andie will find it."

Liz laughed. "I doubt anything is." She could sure use the money, though.

"You might be surprised."

Jane stood there holding the coffee pot, wearing a troubled expression that Liz recognized. It was the same look Liz had had on her face when she was going through everything with her ex.

"I can see something is on your mind. Guy trouble? Sometimes it helps to talk to a stranger who won't spread your business all over town." Liz gestured for Jane to sit across from her.

Jane smiled and sighed. "You're perceptive. It's not really guy trouble… but maybe."

"Tell me all about it."

Jane took a deep breath and put her hand down to pet

Cooper, who had trotted to her side when she sat. "I was married to a wonderful man, but he died many years ago."

Liz felt an immediate pang of sympathy. "Oh, I'm so sorry!"

Jane shook her head. "Like I said, it was long ago, and I have a new man now. One who is kind and sweet."

"But..."

"He wants me to work less. Find someone to take some hours here at Tides. Wants to spend more time together. For some reason, that makes me nervous."

"But you really care about him."

"Very much."

"Woof!"

Liz laughed. "Cooper seems to agree."

"Cooper was actually Mike's dog, but he couldn't have him in the place he was renting here, so I sort of adopted him. Of course, now Mike has a more permanent place in town where he could have Cooper, but Mike likes him to stay at Tides with me. He said that Cooper will protect me. From what, I have no idea, but I love having the dog with me, so I don't question it."

Liz petted the dog. "I bet he would protect you." She looked up at Jane. "It sounds like Mike's a great guy. Do you think you might just be nervous because you lost your first husband so young, and you're afraid that might happen again?"

"Maybe. But that seems so silly. I mean, why would that cause me not to want to hire someone here?"

"Well, if you hire someone to work at Tides, then you

can spend more time with Mike, and your relationship might progress to the next level. Then you would have that much more to lose if anything happened to him."

"Oh. I didn't think of it that way."

"But it sounds like it is all misplaced worry. I would hate to see things get messed up with you and Mike because you're worrying about something that might never happen."

Liz was happy to see the tension in Jane's shoulders ease.

"Thanks. It makes sense now that you put it that way. I guess my subconscious was being overly paranoid. I'll have to try to get it to butt out." Jane studied Liz for a minute. "But I suspect I'm not the only one that might have some misplaced worry. Is there a reason you don't want to stay in your house besides the mess?"

Liz wasn't sure if it was the ocean, the coffee, or the dog, but she found herself telling Jane everything about her past. The way her father had always been so critical. How most of their communication when she was a teen was him yelling. How she'd moved away to college and then stayed away from her father, doing only the minimum at the end. How her husband had frittered away all their money and then dumped her and, finally, how her apartment was being turned into condos, and she couldn't afford any place to live back home.

"So I'll be homeless in a few months."

"You can stay here! I'm sure we'll have plenty of empty rooms."

"Oh, I couldn't impose. But thanks."

"No, thank *you*. You've given me some insight into my issues, and I'm grateful."

"It's my pleasure." Liz took a deep breath. It had felt good to talk to someone about all her issues, even if no solution had resulted. She was happy that she'd given Jane something to think about and truly hoped her relationship with Mike could get to the next level.

Liz finished her coffee and set the mug down. "Well, I'd better get to the house. Who knows—maybe I'll find a rare antique that will solve all my money issues!"

CHAPTER TEN

After Liz left, Jane cleaned up the table and went to the kitchen. She fed Cooper, popped a bagel into the toaster, and sat at the old pine table that had been the setting for many family dinners for generations.

Jane felt bad for Liz, and her offer to stay at Tides was genuine. The inn was usually nearly empty in the late fall and winter. She'd have several empty rooms. It was still a mystery, though, why Liz wouldn't stay in her family home. Her childhood couldn't have been *that* bad. Maybe Liz just needed to see things from a different perspective.

Just like Jane was now seeing things from a different perspective, thanks to her conversation with Liz. Had she been subconsciously procrastinating about hiring someone because she was afraid that spending more time with Mike would lead to something more permanent and she didn't want to lose another person she'd let get so close? Logically she knew that was silly, and knowing that gave her a new focus.

"Time to get out of my comfort zone, Coop." Jane flipped open the paper to the classifieds. Cooper, who was lying by the back door, swished his tail back and forth as if agreeing.

Jane studied the ads to inspire some ad copy ideas that suited her needs, then she called Debbie at the local paper and told her what she wanted.

"Do you want to have them contact you by phone or email?" Debbie asked. "I suggest email. Otherwise, you might have a lot of weirdos calling."

"Weirdos? Does that happen often?" Jane didn't want to have to weed through a bunch of undesirable applicants.

"Sometimes. You know how people are."

"Right. Email it is, then. You wouldn't happen to know anyone who might be interested, do you?" It never hurt to ask around.

"No but I'll keep my eyes peeled and my ears open."

Debbie told her the price for the ad, and Jane gave her the business credit card number and hung up.

Judging by the way Cooper's gaze flicked from Jane to the screen door, he wanted to go for a walk on the beach.

"Okay, buddy. I think I can sneak out for a short walk."

On the beach, Jane took her shoes off and let her feet sink into the soft sand. It was still too early for the sun to have heated it, so the sand was cool, but the rough texture still felt good. Cooper rushed off and returned with a stick. Jane threw it.

Cooper raced to get it. He returned dutifully and dropped it at her feet, looking up at her with a goofy smile on his furry face.

She threw it again, and Cooper raced off again.

They repeated the process as Jane angled down to the water's edge. She couldn't resist dipping a toe in. She jerked her foot back. The water was cold enough to take her breath away. No surprise there. The Maine ocean was ice cold in August, and now, at the end of summer, it was even chillier.

She walked on the hard wet sand at the water's edge, throwing the stick and watching the sandpipers race along the foamy surf. They never seemed to think the water was too cold.

After twenty minutes, she came to the portion of the beach that was dotted with small cottages. She glanced over at the one that Maxi rented as an art studio. Maybe she'd be out on her patio with a coffee, and Jane would drop in for a visit.

Maxi wasn't sipping coffee on the patio, though. Jane saw through the picture window that her friend was in the living room, standing at her easel. As Jane watched, Maxi raced to the couch and picked up Rembrandt. The black cat did not look pleased as Maxi arranged him on the couch then ran back to the easel.

Maxi appeared to be busy, so Jane proceeded down

the beach, enjoying the sunshine and cool ocean breeze, satisfied that she'd taken a solid step toward hiring someone to take some of the workload off her shoulders at Tides.

CHAPTER ELEVEN

*P*ainting a cat was not easy, Maxi thought as she struggled to get Picasso into the perfect position next to Rembrandt. She'd given up on expecting them to sit still while she painted, even though they were quite happy to do that all day long when she wasn't trying to paint them. Now she only wanted them to stay still for a few seconds so she could snap a picture.

She glanced back at the easel. She'd sketched in the scene and painted the background. She'd done a good job portraying Rembrandt's sleek ebony coat and Picasso's snow-white fur and pink nose. But their eyes were dull, not intelligent and mischievous like they were in real life.

Picasso was curled on the chair near the window, basking in the sun. Maxi crept up to him with her cell phone. She crouched down and made a noise so he would open his gorgeous blue eyes, but before she could snap a photo….

Meow!

He bolted from the chair, somehow pushing it back into the window and knocking over a starfish that had been sitting on the windowsill. He stopped in the hallway and looked back at her with reproachful eyes.

"Fine, I'll paint Rembrandt, then, and make him famous."

Rembrandt didn't like that idea. He ran under the couch as she approached while Picasso leapt up on the kitchen counter and started batting at her brushes with his paw.

Her phone trilled. It was her husband, James. Maxi plopped down onto the sofa and answered.

"Hi, honey, how is it going?"

"Exhausting! Turns out herding cats isn't as easy as I thought."

James laughed, which immediately made Maxi feel better. "Sounds like you need a break."

"You can say that again."

"How about we meet at Splash for a glass of wine at four?"

"That sounds absolutely perfect."

Maxi hung up, feeling much better. She and James had gone through a rough spot, but their relationship had come out stronger in the end. And now things were absolutely perfect.

Well, nearly perfect, she thought, as Rembrandt crawled into her lap and stared up at her adoringly as if trying to make up for his previous bad behavior.

"Don't think you can be forgiven so easily," she said then hugged the cat anyway.

CHAPTER TWELVE

The small kitchen area at Curlz, the hair salon across the street from Andie's antique store and apartment, had become almost as familiar to Andie as her own kitchen. She often popped over to chat with Mary when business was slow for them both and she wanted to take break.

Andie settled back in the chair, sipping a peppermint tea while Mary relaxed in between clients.

"So, you have no idea who the Civil War papers belong to?" Mary was always interested in the antiques that Andie bought. "No one in town has that last name?"

"The person I got it from said it was left in their attic. They bought the house as a foreclosure and don't know who owned it before. I tried the bank, but they weren't very helpful."

Mary dipped her teabag into her mug. She had a variety of mugs, and this one was black with white scissors dancing across the rim. "Maybe the family doesn't want them?"

The thought had never occurred to Andie. She couldn't imagine someone not wanting their family history. "Maybe, but I don't feel right just selling them or throwing them away. I think it's more likely that the family didn't know they were up there. The box was probably put there by some ancestor generations ago."

"Yeah, probably." Mary thought for a few minutes. "Lucky for you, I might be able to help. Agnes Crosby works down at the town hall. She comes in every month for a cut and color. Maybe she knows of a way you can find out."

Mary grabbed her phone off the counter and dialed a number. "Agnes? It's Mary over at Curlz. I have a question. If someone wanted to find out who owned a house that had been foreclosed on, could you help them?"

Andie watched as Mary nodded and said "uh-huh" a few times. Then she hung up the phone. "Agnes says that sometimes that information is sealed. She doesn't want to dig in and get into trouble, but she did have another idea. You could trace the family tree."

Andie frowned. "What do you mean?"

"The town library has a huge genealogy section. You can put in your guy's name and see the family tree."

"Really? That will be great. Thanks so much."

"No need to thank me. After all, we're practically family." Mary got a mischievous glint in her gray eyes.

SEASIDE BONDS

"Speaking of which? Is my favorite nephew coming today?"

Andie's cheeks heated, and she felt silly. She was a grown woman, but somehow, thoughts of Shane always made her feel like the teenager she'd been when she'd first met him. It was downright embarrassing. "I'm waiting for him to come and pick me up for dinner, actually."

"Just killing time here with me, then?" Mary feigned being insulted.

Andie laughed. "Oh no. I'm killing time with Shane. Just using a date with him as an excuse to talk to you."

The door opened, and Shane walked in. Andie's heart did a little skip, as it always did when he came into the room. He was tall with dark, slightly graying hair and kind gray eyes. And when he smiled at her, the crinkles at the corners of his eyes didn't make him look aged—they made him look magical.

"Hey, how are my favorite girls?" Shane came over and kissed Mary on the cheek and Andie on the lips.

"Great and you? How are things over at the Brown house?" Andie asked. Shane was a general contractor in town and had been renovating a house for the Brown family. He must've gone home to change and shave because he smelled slightly spicy and looked fresh in a crisp, clean shirt and jeans.

"Pretty good. Got the kitchen in, and the tile guys are coming tomorrow for the bathrooms. I was thinking maybe we could head on over to Splash and watch the sunset. Maybe split some appetizers?"

"Sounds delicious."

Shane turned to Mary. "Would you like to join us?"

Mary waved her hand. "No, you two go along. I don't want to be a third wheel. Besides, I have a client coming in half an hour."

CHAPTER THIRTEEN

A basket with a note from Bunny sat on the front steps to Liz's house.

Thought you might need a snack.

Inside were some muffins that looked freshly baked and tomatoes from her dad's garden. She glanced over at the house next door to see Bunny looking out a window. Liz waved and headed inside. She had to admit she kind of liked the old woman and found it sweet that she'd baked muffins. Ideally, Bunny wouldn't be a pest, though.

Was it her imagination, or did the house smell a little less dusty and mildewy than it had the day before? She flicked the switch on the living room wall, and the lights came on. At least the electric company had been timely in their restoration of service. She moved into the kitchen, taking the basket with her, and cleared a space on the Formica counter.

The blueberry muffins were still warm and smelled of sweetness, and she could practically taste the juicy middles of the bright-red tomatoes. She was surprised at the fond memories the tomatoes brought up. Her dad had always been so proud of his garden. Tomatoes, zucchini, squash, and even cucumbers. One time he'd tried to grow corn, but that hadn't worked out. As a kid, she'd spent a lot of time in the garden with her dad, learning how to plant, fertilize, and harvest. Surprisingly, those memories brought a smile to her lips.

When had her dad become so mean? Thinking back, it seemed to have coincided with her teenage years. How odd that she had happy memories before that. An unsettling thought bubbled up. When her own kids were teenagers, they weren't exactly all sweetness and light. She remembered many fights. Had she been the same to her parents? Probably. And if that was the case, maybe her father wasn't the only one to blame for those bad memories.

No sense in thinking about the past, though. She bit into a muffin and looked around the house. Where to start?

The kitchen would be the most time-consuming. The countertops were cluttered, and the cabinets were stuffed full. At least her brother had cleaned out the refrigerator and unplugged it before her dad went into assisted living.

She shuddered to think of what six years of moldy food would be like in there.

She started with the cabinets near the fridge, pulling out baking dishes, pots, pans, and cast-iron skillets. Hadn't she read somewhere those could be worth money? Maybe she should set some of the stuff aside and consult Andie before she had it hauled away as junk.

The thought of finding something valuable excited her. She could really use the money, though, of course, she would have to split it with her siblings. Truth be told, she felt like she should get a higher percentage, since she was doing the bulk of the work, but she hadn't wanted to broach that topic with her brother and sister. Things had been a bit strained among the three of them because they hadn't agreed on their father's care or what to do with the house. The funeral had brought them back together, and she didn't want to mess that up now. Besides, she really didn't have anything better to do.

Moving on to the drawers, she opened the old bread box and slid the metal top back. She was a little worried she might find old moldy bread in there, but she didn't. Apparently, her dad had stashed all her mom's old recipe books and cards in there.

She brought them to the kitchen table, cleared a spot, and sat down. The cookbooks were stuffed full of magazine articles, and the recipe cards were in her mom's own handwriting, the ink faded and the cards splotched with food stains. They included some of her favorite dishes from when she was a kid—crab puffs, cherry cheesecake pie, Congo bars. Warm memories of cooking in the kitchen with her mom bubbled up.

She was so engrossed looking through the recipes she didn't notice Bunny until she heard a knock at the door.

Bunny was wearing what looked like a flowered house coat and furry pink slippers. Liz couldn't help the expression on her face when she opened the door.

Bunny laughed. "We don't stand much on formality here in the neighborhood. Pajamas are not uncommon."

"You mean you walk around like this?" Liz asked, glancing out to the street, expecting to see an army of neighbors in furry slippers.

Bunny shrugged. "Sometimes. We've all been here a long time, and we're kind of like family. Your dad was too."

Liz definitely couldn't picture her father trotting around the neighborhood in pajamas, but the thought of neighbors as close as family tugged at her heartstrings. It would be nice to have a neighborhood of family. A place to belong and where people watched out for one another. She hadn't had that since her kids were little and her marriage was solid.

But then came the disturbing thought that she actually didn't have any place to live now. All her belongings were in storage. And after she was done cleaning out her dad's house, where would she go?

Staying at Tides had actually brought a newfound appreciation for her old hometown. Living near the beach was always nice, but she couldn't afford a place in

Lobster Bay. Maybe a neighboring town? Of course, she would never take Jane up on her offer to stay at Tides over the winter.

Bunny came in, and they sat at the table. "Thanks for the muffins. Would you like one?"

"You're very welcome, dear. I guess I could have one." She produced a stick of butter and some tea bags from her pocket. "I came prepared."

Liz rummaged up her mother's old stainless steel kettle and boiled some water.

"So, how is the cleanup going?" Bunny gestured to the piles of items Liz had taken out of the cupboards.

"Pretty good. I think there's a lot of junk. I might have to get a dumpster."

"Don't be too hasty. Your dad didn't throw anything away, which I guess is obvious. But you don't want to let go of some of these things from your childhood because you can never get them back." Bunny suddenly looked very sad. "I should know."

"Oh?" Liz sensed Bunny wanted to talk about it, so she bit into the muffin she'd just slathered with butter and settled back in her chair.

"Yep. My family home burned down when I was young. We had generations of antiques and things in there, but nothing was saved." Bunny got a faraway look in her eyes. "There was one distant relative that had taken some of my great-grandparents' things, but he had a falling out with my dad, and we never got anything back."

Liz frowned. "Oh, that's so sad. I'm sorry. What

happened?" Liz thought about Tides and all the generations of family belongings there. Jane seemed so happy to be surrounded by them. But those things were much older than anything in this house. Her family didn't have any antiques from the early 1900s and certainly nothing expensive. But the items that filled the house still elicited a warm feeling of nostalgia, even though they were only from the fifties through eighties.

"Ack. Too much drama. Something about family trees and names." Bunny leaned forward. Family history is important, and you don't want to let go of it too easily." She looked pointedly around the kitchen.

Liz followed her gaze. The kitchen was a mess, but some of the items did bring back fond family memories. Like her mother's recipes and the vintage kitchen canisters with colorful mushrooms on them.

"Of course, one can't keep everything. Maybe you could donate some of the things you don't want?" Bunny's words brought Liz out of her thoughts. "Like all the books in the den? Your dad loved reading, and I have to say he did collect a ton of books over the years. But the library is always looking for good books. I hope you're not going to just throw those out."

"No, of course not. I'll stop by the library later and see if they want them. And maybe the Salvation Army?"

"That's my girl." Bunny shoved the rest of the muffin into her mouth and stood. "Well, I'll leave you to it. Let me know if you need anything. I'm right next door."

Bunny left, and Liz continued her task. She was

surprised to find herself humming as she boxed up some of the books and set the items she thought might be valuable aside for Andie.

Time flew by, and soon it was late afternoon. Funny, she hadn't hated being there as much as she thought she would, but now that it was time for a break, she needed a real meal. Muffins and tomatoes weren't cutting the mustard.

She grabbed the tomatoes on her way out the door. There were far too many for her to eat. Maybe Jane could use some at the inn.

CHAPTER FOURTEEN

Splash was one of Maxi's favorite restaurants because the outdoor patio area sat right on the beach. It wasn't anything fancy, but who cared? The view was amazing, and even though the sun set behind them in the west, the ocean was still dazzling with the reflection of pinks, blues, and golds.

The menu was decent enough. She liked the appetizers, and you could get a good drink, like the gin and tonic she had sitting in front of her right now. After a stressful day, nothing soothed her more than listening to the ocean while she watched the seagulls darting around on the beach for scraps.

Even this late in the season and at this time of day, there were still some holdouts on the beach with their coolers and colorful umbrellas. Despite the cooler air, children rushed screeching into the waves farther down the beach.

She settled back in her seat and smiled at James. "Thanks so much for suggesting this. It's just what I needed."

He put his hand over hers. "I'm always happy to dine with my favorite girl. But I feel bad that the painting is giving you trouble. Is there anything I can do to help?"

Maxi shook her head. "I wish. It's just that I can't seem to capture the look in Goblin's eyes. I am making some progress by practicing on the cats, but it's impossible to get them to stay still enough."

"Maybe I could hold them for you?" James suggested.

"What? No. You're busy at work. I don't want to bother you with it." Maxi was warmed by his suggestion. The old James would never have offered to miss work, much less risk getting cat hair all over him.

"It's no problem. I have some vacation days that I have to use anyway, and what better place than at the cottage on the beach with you and the cats."

"Well, if you're sure…" Maxi supposed it would help. She didn't usually like painting in front of people, but James was different. And it would be nice to spend some time with him in the cottage.

"That settles it, then." James pulled his hand away and picked up his beer, and she missed the warmth of his touch. "I'll come tomorrow whenever you want and hold them."

"Fancy meeting you here!" The familiar voice pulled Maxi's gaze from her husband, and she looked over to see Andie and Shane standing at their table.

"I didn't know you guys were coming here tonight." Maxi gestured toward the extra chairs at the table. "Why don't you join us?"

"Well, if you're sure we're not interrupting?" Andie's gaze skipped from Maxi to James.

James stood and pulled out a chair for her. "Not at all, we're always happy to eat with you guys."

Kristi, the waitress, came over with four extra place settings.

"I don't think we need all these," Maxi said. "There's only four of us, and James and I already have ours."

Kristi jerked her head toward the front of the restaurant. "I just saw Claire and Rob come in, so I assumed they'd be joining you."

Maxi craned her head in that direction. "Oh, there they are. Good thinking." She motioned to Claire and Rob, and they cut through the crowd that was waiting to be seated.

They were all settled in and just about to order when Andie spotted Jane and Mike walking down the beach with Cooper.

"Oh, look! Let's see if we can get them to join us." Andie stood and yelled across the beach, catching their attention.

Jane and Mike came to the edge of the patio.

"I didn't know we were having a couples' night," Jane said.

Maxi knew Jane was joking. Of course they wouldn't have a couples' night and leave Jane and Mike out. "We all ran into each other by accident. There's plenty of chairs at the table. Can you guys join us?"

Luckily, the round tables outside on the patio were all very large, and since it was outdoors, dogs were allowed. Jane and Mike accepted the offer, and everyone settled in, ordering a round of drinks and appetizers.

"How funny that we all ended up here." Shane raised his glass. "Here's to impromptu dinners on the beach."

"Might be one of the last ones." Jane zipped up her hoodie. "It's getting chilly at night."

"We better make the most of it while we still have warm weather. But how did you get away, Jane?" Claire asked.

"Liz brought a bunch of tomatoes from the garden at her house, and Brenda is making a frittata with them tomorrow morning. She wanted to do some prep work tonight, so she said she'd watch the place. Liz is our only guest, and no one new is scheduled to check in, so it should be pretty easy."

"A frittata?" Mike's brows shot up. "I'll be over first thing in the morning."

"It is nice to get out. So I'm really focusing on my hunt for someone to take some shifts at Tides now," Jane said as Kristie slid calamari, steamers, and fish dip onto their table.

"Did you say you're hiring at Tides?" Kristi asked Jane then blushed. "Sorry, I couldn't help but overhear."

"It's no problem. I'm looking for someone to work part-time."

"My cousin has been looking for something. Could I have her call or drop in?"

Jane looked a little hesitant, but Mike spoke up.

"That sounds perfect, doesn't it?" He looked at Jane.

"Yes. I suppose it does." Jane picked a clam out of its shell and swirled it in the broth. "Maybe she could stop by tomorrow. I'll be there all morning."

"Okay. Thanks, I'll tell her." Kristi left.

"I think it's great that you are starting to look for help," Claire said. "You won't regret hiring someone. I love having Hailey to depend on, and Rob loves Tillie and Ella. It gives us more of a chance to be together."

The two of them smiled at each other so brightly that Maxi nearly heard wedding bells.

She was glad Jane was thinking about getting help. It would be good for Andie too. They both worked so hard, and Jane deserved to spend more time with Mike. Maxi remembered helping Jane through that horrible first year after her husband died. And she'd always tried to encourage Jane to date again years afterward, but she'd never found anyone until Mike. Mike was obviously smitten with Jane. Spending more time together would be a good thing for them both.

Maxi spread some fish dip on a cracker. She was content to eat good food on the beach with her best friends. Now, if only she could nail down the painting, everything would be perfect.

CHAPTER FIFTEEN

Kristie's cousin must have really wanted a job because she called Tides first thing the next morning and arranged to come in for an interview.

They were sitting in the dining room, which was still much the same as it had been when Jane's grandparents were alive. A long mahogany table was set up in the middle, surrounded by smaller round tables. The walls, covered in floral wallpaper, boasted gilt-framed paintings and floor-to-ceiling windows with the drapes pulled back to expose the ocean view. A heavily carved server, where Brenda set out the breakfast dishes when the inn was full, sat along one wall. Since the only people in the dining room this morning were Jane, Liz, and Brenda, they hadn't bothered with setting things out. The three of them had eaten in the kitchen. Brenda's frittatas loaded with the tomatoes from Liz's garden had been delicious, and Jane was very full.

Stacy sat across the table from Jane. She was an interesting individual with lots of piercings and tattoos. Jane didn't really mind them, but her guests skewed older, and she wondered if that might be a problem. Not to mention she was wearing a ripped T-shirt and shorts. Jane hadn't thought about having a dress code, but perhaps she should mention the idea.

"Do you have any experience with registering guests? Maybe a motel or something?" Jane asked.

Stacy blew a bubble and then sucked it in and continued chomping as she answered. "I was head hostess at the Waffle House."

"Head hostess? That's great." Jane was trying to be positive. "Though I suppose it's a little different than checking guests into their rooms, still I'm sure you could be trained."

Stacy laughed. "Trained? It hardly seems like you need to be a rocket scientist."

Jane frowned. Wasn't that a little mean? "Still, there are some things to learn. How do you feel about working weekends?"

Stacy looked taken aback. "Weekends? I thought this was just part-time?"

"It is, but that includes weekends. I'll be here mostly during the week, and we need someone to fill in a few afternoons and on weekends."

Stacy chomped her gum harder. "I don't know about that. I have a lot of plans on the weekends."

Jane set the sparse resume Stacy had given her on the table and sat back in her chair. "Perhaps this job isn't a good fit for you, then?"

Stacy's face changed as if she was just realizing the same thing. "Yeah, maybe not. But I really need a job. Is there any way you could change the hours for me?"

"Afraid not. We really need someone on the weekends." Jane stood, hoping Stacy would follow her lead. "I have your number, though, and if we change our minds, I'll call you."

"Oh. Okay. Thanks."

She walked Stacy out and then collapsed into one of the chairs in the parlor. Cooper trotted along behind her and sat looking up at her with sympathy in his eyes.

"Yeah, that wasn't what I expected either." Jane rubbed behind his ears.

Andie stuck her head into the parlor. "Was that your interviewee?"

"Yep."

"That bad, huh?"

Jane sighed. Maybe she was expecting too much? "I guess I don't know what my expectations are. She seemed kind of young."

"Well, if that's what she wears to an interview, things have changed a lot since I interviewed." Andie sat on the sofa across from her. "Maybe we need to set some guidelines? What exactly are we looking for?"

"Well, definitely someone responsible. Some kind of experience would be a plus, but I think the job is pretty easy to learn."

Andie nodded. "And somebody who has a pleasant demeanor for the guests."

"Right, and maturity."

"And can make decisions without calling us all the time."

"Agreed." Jane felt better. "What brings you here?"

"I was just on my way to the library and figured I'd stop in and see if you needed anything. I'm going to look up the genealogy on the Civil War guy."

"That's a good idea. Hope you find something."

"Me too. I mean, I guess if the family hasn't missed it all these years, they probably don't even know the papers and uniform exist, but I would really like to get the items back to them."

Jane nodded. "That was fun last night with all of us running in to each other at Splash. We should plan more get-togethers with the eight of us."

"I agree. I really love our morning coffees, but it would be fun to have something that we do regularly with the guys too." They'd gotten together many times but had nothing planned on a regular basis.

"It's a great way to catch up. Poor Maxi, though. She seems a little down. She's still having trouble with the dog painting." Jane reached down and petted Cooper, who responded by thumping his tail against the leg of the table.

"She'll work it out. She's a great artist."

"Yep, she just needs to figure it out."

"Speaking of get-togethers, we're meeting at Sandcastles tomorrow morning, right?"

"Yes." Jane's phone pinged and Andie stood.

"I gotta get to the library. See you later."

Jane looked down at her phone and saw an email, an applicant replying to her ad in the newspaper. She hoped this one would be a little more suitable.

CHAPTER SIXTEEN

"Get back here, you little rascal!" James watched Rembrandt dive under the couch until only his black tail stuck out.

"Maybe it will be easier to catch Picasso," Maxi suggested.

James had been trying to wrangle the two cats into submission for over an hour. Unfortunately, the two fur balls objected vehemently to doing anything Maxi and James wanted them to do. On any other day, they were happy to lounge around in one spot, soaking in the sun all day, and even happier if they could be on someone's lap. But not now. They had an uncanny ability to sense that was exactly what James and Maxi wanted and were now determined to do the exact opposite.

James turned and eyed the white cat, who looked at him warily. He took a step. Picasso's fluffy tail swished. He lunged and grabbed the cat.

Picasso wriggled in James's arms. "Meow!"

"Want a treat?" Maxi rushed in, holding a piece of the cats' favorite tuna-flavored treat.

That caught their attention. Picasso stopped wriggling and sniffed. Rembrandt poked his head out from under the couch.

"I guess we know how to control them." James carefully sat down with Picasso in his lap, and Maxi handed him the bag of treats.

Not to be left out, Rembrandt jumped up onto the couch. James managed to arrange both cats in his lap and keep them there with the aid of the treats.

"We might have to put them on a diet after this," Maxi joked as she got to work behind the easel. Pictures were great, but there was nothing like painting from real life. She could capture the shadows of light, the subtle change in colors. Soon she was lost in the art of painting.

After about an hour, Maxi stepped back from the painting. "There. I think I got enough for now. I can put the final details in later but won't need you to sit with the cats."

James got up from the chair and brushed the fur off. He stood beside her at the easel. "The fur is really good. You really captured it."

"Thanks to you." She kissed him on the cheek, happy she'd made progress. The painting of the two cats curled up together was good. The contrast of the white and black fur was striking.

She put the brush in the small glass jar of turpentine

and stashed it in the cupboard so the cats couldn't get into it. "I think it's coming along. After I take a break, I'll work on the eyes more, but I'm happy with the way they are coming out."

"How about we go for a walk." James looked toward the beach. It was a gorgeous sunny day and perfect weather for walking. Even better, the beach was empty. They would have it all to themselves.

"Great idea." Maxi took off her painter's smock and draped it over one of the kitchen chairs. A picture of Goblin caught her eye. Bert and Harry had given it to her for the painting. Their favorite picture of the dog, it featured Goblin looking up at the camera with her wrinkled fawn-and-brown face, pug nose, and expressive brown eyes.

Even through the photograph, Maxi could see the love in the dog's eyes, and it made her heart melt. She just *had* to get this painting right for Bert and Harry.

CHAPTER SEVENTEEN

The Lobster Bay library was in a large gothic stone building that had an arched oak door with iron hinges. Walking into the library felt like entering an old castle. Inside, the ceilings were vaulted, and the air was heavy with silence. A bespectacled librarian sat behind a large round oak desk, stacks of returned books in carts behind her.

"Can you tell me where the genealogy section is?" Andie asked in a whisper.

"We have books on genealogy and also a local history section."

"The local history is what I'm after."

"You're looking something up?"

"Yes."

The librarian nodded as if she was expecting that and had just been testing her. "Everything we have is on microfilm. We're just a small operation and don't have staff to get everything online."

"I understand." That was too bad because it would have been a lot easier to sit at home and look things up.

"You'll find that section in the basement." She stood and pointed to the left. "Around that corner there and down the steps."

"Thanks."

The basement was not as nice as the upper level. The floor was old green and beige tile, the walls an uninspiring off-white like the color of manilla folders. The old gray metal cabinets were clearly labeled, and she found the town genealogy records easily. The microfilm machines sat in a dark corner, each one in its own little cubby. Andie sat down with several rolls of film and got to work.

After a few hours, her eyes were burning from scrolling through the old documents, which included images of certificates and newspaper announcements with births, deaths, and marriages.

There was no way to search, so she had to look through each roll. She didn't find anything for the name Koslachowski, but most of the information was dated from the 1890s and on. He might have moved out of town by then, or maybe he wasn't even from Lobster Bay. Just because the box was in an attic in one of the houses in town didn't mean it had been there since the end of the Civil War.

She made some notes about what rolls she'd searched

and put everything away. Her eyes weren't that young anymore, and she needed a break. She could come back later and dig further, though she didn't have high hopes of finding anything in the other films.

In the lobby, Andie spotted Liz standing at the round desk with several boxes of books. "How's the cleanup going?"

The librarian jerked her attention from the book she was processing to frown at her. Oops. Andie guessed she hadn't lowered her voice enough.

"Good." Liz whispered. "Better than I thought. My dad was a big reader, so I'm donating these books."

Andie glanced into the box, which contained mostly fiction. Nothing too old or leather bound in there, so Liz wasn't giving away anything valuable.

"I also found some items I thought you might be interested in. Do you want to come and look at them?"

That perked Andie up. "I'd love to. What have you got?"

"Some kitchenware. I heard it could be valuable, and there's a whole china cabinet of dishes and knickknacks."

"Sounds like fun. When were you thinking?"

"I have a few more rooms to clean out, so I was thinking it would be best if you wait until I have it all sorted. Maybe Thursday?"

"Sounds perfect."

They set a time, and Andie left, much to the relief of the librarian, who looked like she'd been just about to shush them. Andie was disappointed that she hadn't found out more about her Civil War guy, but at least she could look forward to checking out Liz's antiques.

CHAPTER EIGHTEEN

After Liz dropped off the books, she picked up a lobster roll and returned to the house. She'd cleared some space off the kitchen table earlier, so she sat down and bit into the sweet buttery sandwich. It was just the way she liked it—a buttered, grilled hot dog bun with nothing inside except lobster meat, mayo, and crispy iceberg lettuce.

As she looked around, a feeling of nostalgia crept in. She smiled, remembering fighting with Shelly and Peter over who would wash the dishes and who would dry. Nights at this very table playing Scrabble with the whole family. Now that she'd cleared out the dust and clutter, the house wasn't too bad. It had been kept up nicely, and she liked the retro feel.

Her phone blared.

"Peter! How are you?" Liz had only talked to her

brother once since the funeral and was genuinely happy to hear from him.

"Good. You? Shelly said you were working on the house already."

"Yep. Cleaned out some junk. Boy, was it full."

Peter sighed. "I know. I'm sorry about that. Dad couldn't keep up with it, and I guess none of us noticed. When he had the stroke and I came in to close things up, I was shocked. I guess I should have cleaned up, but I was more worried about getting back to the hospital. We didn't even know for a while if he would make it."

"You did the right thing," Liz assured him, just as she always did.

"So it's not too much work? I could get some time off—"

"It's fine," Liz interrupted him. Now that she was in a groove, she didn't want anyone coming in and messing with her process. She wanted to do things on her own timeline.

"Okay. What about all the stuff. Are you dumping it? Do we need to do any repairs or fix things up for sale? There's still a little bit in Dad's savings, so let me know if you need it."

"Thanks, I actually might be able to sell some of this old stuff. Believe it or not."

"Really?"

She told him about Andie and how she'd volunteered to take a look. "If it turns out there's a million-dollar masterpiece in the attic or something, you'll find me on a tropical beach," Liz joked.

"We can only wish! But if there is anything of value, you can keep the money. You're doing all the work."

"I wouldn't dream of it. I'll put it into any repairs." It was nice of him to offer, but Liz didn't need handouts like that.

They chatted a bit about their families, and then Liz got back to work. She wanted to go through most of the closets and drawers and pull out anything she thought Andie might be interested in. Some things she didn't want to let go of, like the vintage silver flatware her mother always put out on holidays and the living room lamp that had been her favorite.

She found the old photo album in the cabinet next to the fireplace. She was almost afraid to open it, worrying that it would bring up bad memories and ruin her good mood. But as she sat on the sofa and flipped the pages, she began reliving happy times.

Photos of her and her siblings when they were little. The yard looked so strange, since it had hardly any trees back then. The giant maple was much smaller too.

Thanksgivings with the table loaded with a giant turkey and all the fixings. The big tree her dad would drag home every Christmas loaded with tinsel and those giant bulb lights they had in those days. And the toys! Dolls, play kitchen sets, trucks. If only some of those were still around, they'd probably be worth a bundle. But they'd been well played with and tossed or given to younger cousins decades ago.

She paused at one photo. A picture of her with the German shepherd mix, Ranger, they'd had when she was eleven. In the photo, she was sitting on the grass with Ranger right beside her. Her hand was on his back, and they were both smiling at the camera. She remembered that day and the warm reassuring feeling of Ranger's back as if it were yesterday.

How nice would it be to have a dog now? She was sort of lonely. Her kids called frequently but rarely came to visit. Her daughter, Sophie, was busy with her own toddler, and her son, Matt, was away half the year on a crab fishing boat.

But before she could get a dog, she needed a place to live.

But where? She wasn't tied to her old town. In fact, she wanted to be far from it, since Kyle had settled near there. She needed a change. Someplace friendly. Near the beach would be nice. A small town like this one, with a garden and neighbors that were like family.

Her thoughts were interrupted by a knock on the door. It was Bunny. Liz invited her in, and they sat on the living room sofa.

"So, tell me more about this neighborhood." Liz put on some tea while Bunny talked about each house, who had lived there in the past, and who lived there currently. It was easy to see why Bunny loved living in the neighborhood. As she talked, Liz started to form a plan.

CHAPTER NINETEEN

Sandcastles was as busy as usual when the four met for coffee the next morning. The bright sun had chased away the worst of the morning chill, and Claire, Maxi, Jane, and Andie took a table outside, even though the weather was still a bit brisk. Inside, the chatter of customers wafted out the door whenever Hailey came out to refill their coffee mugs.

"Brrr…" Maxi pulled her white waffle sweater tighter around her.

"Won't be long until there's a layer of frost in the morning." Andie shivered.

"Then the trees will start to turn. That's always pretty and brings in leaf-peeping tourists," Claire said.

"And then, after that, snow!" Jane sounded happy about that, and the others stared at her. "What? It's pretty on the beach and makes the town look like a Hallmark movie."

"I guess it does have its appeal." Maxi picked a corn muffin off the tray of pastries that Claire had set in the middle of the table. She tried to feed a tiny piece to Cooper, who was sitting between her and Jane, when Jane stopped her.

"I think Cooper has been getting enough treats," Jane said kindly. "Liz has been feeding him snacks at Tides. He needs to keep his trim figure."

Maxi made a sympathetic face at the dog, who was looking up at her with eager brown eyes. "Sorry, buddy, looks like you're on a diet." She turned to Jane. "Speaking of Liz, how is your guest?"

"She's great. She seems to have bonded with Cooper and said he reminded her of the dog she used to have." Jane stirred cream into her coffee. "She does seem a bit lonely."

Claire frowned. "Why is she staying at Tides? Her house is right in town. Seems more convenient to stay there."

Jane shrugged. "Bad childhood memories."

"Good thing we don't have those, it would be hard to run the inn." Andie smiled at Jane over the rim of her mug.

"Darn tootin'—your folks were salt of the earth. Addie still is." Sally Littlefield had been up on a ladder, fixing part of the awning. She'd known their parents. Heck, she knew most of the people in town. She smiled down at them then zeroed in on Andie. "What's with the scowl on your face?"

"Who, me?" Andie didn't realize she'd been scowling. Truth was, though, her mind wasn't totally on the conversation. Talk of Liz had gotten her excited about going to see her family treasures, but then that had reminded her of the Civil War soldier she'd had no luck in tracing. "Oh, it's nothing."

"Still no luck finding your Civil War guy?" Claire asked.

"Unfortunately, no."

Sally came down from the ladder and stood beside the table, wiping her hands on a towel. "What's this about a Civil War guy?"

Andie told her about the find from the estate.

"Did you look in the Civil War archives over in Arundel?"

Andie paused. "There's a place that specializes in Civil War data?"

"Yep, got all kinds of information on the battles and soldiers. Names, dates, and descendants." Sally started packing up her tools. "It's all fixed, Claire. I'll send you a bill at the end of the month."

"Great. Thanks!"

"She's a real gem." Jane and Andie had hired Sally to do a lot of work at Tides. "If only I could find someone like Sally to run the inn."

"Kristie's cousin didn't work out?" Claire asked.

Jane snorted. "She was a little… modern for my taste. And then someone emailed me from the classified ad I took out but then never showed for the interview."

"Aww... Don't worry, you'll find someone."

"Morning, ladies!" Bert and Henry stopped by the table, a look of sad longing in their eyes as they stooped to pet Cooper. The stooping came with some creaking and groaning. The two men had to be pushing eighty, but they were the sweetest men in town.

Bert glanced up at Maxi. "How's the portrait going?"

Maxi's stomach plummeted. She didn't have the heart to disappoint them with the truth.

"Great, won't be long now." She tried to keep the smile plastered on her face and stop her panic from bubbling up.

"We can't wait to see it." Bert stood and then helped Harry. "But don't let us rush you."

"Don't worry, I won't. I'm taking my time to get it just perfect."

"That's what we want. Have a nice day, ladies."

After the two men ambled off, everyone turned to Maxi.

"So, you've made a breakthrough with the painting. I knew you could do it," Jane said.

"Hardly, I just couldn't disappoint them." Maxi hated the look of sympathy in their eyes.

Luckily, that didn't last long because Jane's phone pinged. She looked down at it. "Just got an email. Another applicant. This one is older. I hope she'll fit the bill."

CHAPTER TWENTY

After breakfast, Jane went to visit her mother at Tall Pines, and Andie went to relieve Brenda from duty at Tides. Even though she was eager to get to Arundel and see what the Civil War archives had, that would have to wait. Ideally, they'd find someone to work at Tides soon, maybe even the person who had emailed Jane at breakfast.

When she arrived at the inn, Brenda and Liz were chatting it up with a middle-aged couple in the foyer. The woman, who wore a soft blue sweater and jeans and had a designer suitcase beside her, was laughing. The husband, wearing a sky-blue golf shirt and chinos, was enjoying one of Brenda's cookies.

"This is such a lovely inn. I know our stay will be so much fun. Will you be here for breakfast tomorrow, Liz?"

Liz smiled. "You bet. Brenda makes the best breakfasts. Eggs, bacon. Sometimes there's homemade bread. You'll love it."

Brenda handed over the key, and the woman turned to Liz. "And thank you for advice on our daughters. You made me see things a different way."

Liz beamed, and Andie waited for the couple to go upstairs. When they did, she asked, "What was that about?"

Liz shrugged. "They used to bring their kids here when they were little and seemed a bit sad about how their daughters don't have time for them. I gave them a way to see it from the daughters' side."

"People seem to really open up when they are booking a room." Brenda glanced up the stairs. The look on her face indicated she wasn't on board with people blurting out problems to strangers.

Andie was glad they had another guest, and she supposed it was true that people did seem to open up when booking a room. "You can say that again. But you didn't have to feel like you had to give them advice, Liz."

"Oh, no problem. I just blurted it out. Hope you don't mind. Must be my guidance counselor background."

"I'm glad she was here." Brenda came out from behind the desk and took off her apron. "They needed someone to talk to, and I'm better at cooking than talking. Speaking of which, I gotta run. I'm baking cookies with my granddaughter today and need to get to the store."

Andie gave her a hug. "Thanks for watching the front desk."

"I'm happy to do it."

"I better get going too," Liz said. "Are you going to stop by later? I've set some items aside for you."

"Yes, I can't wait." Andie figured she could go after her trip out to Arundel.

Liz gave her the address and left. Liz seemed a lot happier than she had before. Cleaning out her parents' house must not be as bad as she'd expected it to be.

The couple upstairs was getting settled in their room. The place was quiet. Andie went into the front parlor and picked a chocolate kiss out of Grandma's cut glass bowl. She unwrapped the chocolate and popped it into her mouth. The steady tick of the grandfather clock marked the slowly passing time. Only two hours until Jane would be back to relieve her, and she could head out to Arundel and continue her search for her Civil War soldier's family.

CHAPTER TWENTY-ONE

Maxi stood at Bunny Howard's front door clutching her blue-and-white-striped tote and waiting for her to answer. After seeing Bert and Harry at Sandcastles, she'd realized she needed to do everything she could to finish that painting, so she'd dug out the card Muriel had given her and called.

Maxi had never really taken lessons. Art sort of came naturally to her. But Bunny had sounded very nice, and she was looking forward to hearing her advice. Ideally, the lesson would go well.

The door opened to reveal a cheerful senior citizen who was about a foot shorter than Maxi. She was wearing a loose, paint-covered smock and white cotton pants. Her gray hair was up in a messy bun. Maxi liked her right away.

"Maxi? Bunny smiled and opened the door. "Come in.

I've seen your work at the gallery, and it's quite amazing, so I was surprised when you called for a lesson."

Maxi felt a rush of pride at the compliment. It had taken her a long time to be able to accept compliments gracefully. "Thank you. I have a specific problem, and Muriel said you might be able to help me."

"Ahh, well, she would know. Why don't you sit down for some coffee and tell me about the problem?"

Bunny led her through the tidy living room. Though the older, ranch-style house was small, it seemed bigger because Bunny had kept the decor in light whites and beiges and had furniture with simple lines. Unlike most older people's houses, Bunny's residence was not cluttered with "stuff."

The Danish modern dining room table was already set with cups and saucers and a little plate of shortbread cookies. The earthy smell of coffee wafted out from an old-school percolator on the sideboard.

Beyond the dining room, Maxi could see a sunroom that had probably been an addition. This room had several sets of sliding glass doors to let in maximum light and was where Bunny had set up two easels and paint supplies. It looked out over her backyard and the woods beyond as well as the neighbor's yard, which had a large garden that appeared to be somewhat out of control.

Maxi told Bunny about the commission to paint Goblin and the problem she was having capturing the dog's likeness. She'd brought one of her earlier attempts at painting Goblin as well as a practice painting of Rembrandt and Picasso and showed them to Bunny.

Bunny studied the canvases and nodded. "I see. It's the light in the eyes. That makes them come alive. Come on, I'll show you."

At the easel, Bunny sketched in the head of a dog then added fur with quick brush strokes. "This is just a simple sketch for context. I'll go into more detail when I get to the eye, since that's where I think your problem stems from."

A few strokes of the brush later, Bunny had a pretty good rendition of a dog's eye on the canvas.

"See, you use the reflection to give it depth," Bunny said as she added a white dot to the corner of the eye.

Maxi nodded.

"And I always mix at least five colors into the iris." Bunny added some blobs of blue, green, and yellow paint to her pallet and painstakingly added them to the iris area. She stood back and waved at Maxi's canvas. "Now you try."

Maxi picked up the brush, and the two women painted side by side with Bunny instructing. Soon Maxi was lost in the creative act, absorbing all of Bunny's instructions and thinking about how she could apply them to the painting of Goblin.

After an hour, Bunny put down her brush and stretched. "Well, I think that's enough for today. You're coming along, don't you think?"

"I do. Thanks so much." Maxi stepped back to admire her work, her eyes drifting to the garden next door. "I love this room. And the backyard is so scenic. Looks like your neighbor needs to do some yard work, though."

"That's Frank Weston's house. He got sick, and it's been empty for some time. I was keeping the garden going in case he got better. Sadly, he died, and his daughter is cleaning it out."

That sounded like Jane's guest at Tides. "Is her name Liz?"

Bunny looked surprised. "Yes, do you know her?"

"Not really. I knew the family a bit from growing up in town but not well. She's staying at Tides, and my friend Jane runs the inn, so she mentioned her to me." Maxi walked over to the window to view the garden area more closely. This late in the season, most of the plants were dying off, but she could see some bright-red tomatoes waiting to be picked and some pumpkins just getting started. "I wonder why she doesn't stay at the house instead of Tides?"

"I wondered that too. I've chatted to her a bit. Seems like a nice lady, but if you ask me, she has some unresolved issues from her youth."

Maxi turned to face Bunny. "That sounds serious."

"It's not, really. I think she might be making a mountain out of a molehill and misremembering. Frank told me that for some reason, she got cold toward him when she left home for college. Poor Frank. He loved her so much and blamed himself for pushing her too hard in high school. He always just wanted her to succeed. Wanted the best for her. I think she might have been a bit too headstrong. You know how teenagers are."

Maxi thought about her own kids and their high school days. Luckily, they had been good students, but there were times when she'd had to play the bad guy and they'd fought it. They'd had more than their share of arguments. Was that the only reason Liz hadn't wanted to stay in the house, or did Bunny not know the whole story? "That's too bad. I hope she makes her peace."

"Me too. She seems to be coming around. One really needs to hold onto family and treasure it. Once you lose that connection, it's hard to get back." Bunny looked sad for a few seconds then brightened and turned to the paintings. "Let's sign our paintings and clean up. I think you did a great job."

Maxi signed her last name. She'd never been able to come up with a snazzy-looking signature and admired Bunny's, which looked like a squiggle that resembled a K connected to an S.

"Thanks for the lesson. I feel like I connected some dots, but maybe I need a bit more instruction. Can I come back another time?"

"Of course. Why don't you go home and process what you learned? Then you can come back, and we can go deeper into the concepts."

Maxi paid Bunny and carefully laid her wet canvas in

the back of her car. A new sense of hope sprang up inside her. She'd gotten some great tips from Bunny and was becoming more confident that she could do justice to Goblin's likeness.

CHAPTER TWENTY-TWO

Liz shoved the old bedding, placemats, and Tupperware lids that had no bottoms into a garbage bag, which she then put outside the slider to be taken to the end of the driveway for trash collection. Had her father never thrown anything out? She had to admit the place was shaping up. It actually looked good enough to live in.

Sure, it was a little dated, but some of the old lamps and clocks and even the furniture were coming back in style.

But while the inside was shaping up, the outside was another story. She wandered out into the garden, letting old memories wash over her. She laughed when she passed the spot where her dad tried to plant carrots one year. The ground was hard, and the carrots had come out more like disks.

She paused at the heirloom tomato plant and picked

one. Her mouth watered as she imagined sprinkling salt on it and biting into it like an apple as she'd done when she was a kid. Not too much salt now, though. She had to watch her blood pressure.

As she lugged the trash around the side of the house, she spotted Bunny in her sunroom, painting. The older woman was starting to grow on her, and Liz almost looked forward to her visits now. She'd told her all about the other neighbors.

The divorced single mother, Emma Chamberlain, who lived in the modest ranch at number nine. Sheila and Bob Donahue, the middle-aged empty-nesters who lived at number six. Olga Svenson, the ninety-five-year-old woman, proud of her Scandinavian heritage, who delivered Norwegian goodies to them at Christmas and refused to move no matter how much her kids tried to talk her into it. The whole neighborhood watched out for her. It seemed like a good place to live.

And now that the house wasn't such a mess, she might be able to save the estate some money and stay here instead of Tides. She didn't dread coming here anymore. Somehow all the bad memories were being replaced with good ones. Maybe her aged brain had forgotten the wounds of her teenage years... or maybe those wounds had been exaggerated in her head the whole time. Whatever the reason, the house now felt warm and welcoming, like home.

Staying at Tides right on the beach was pretty nice, though. She smiled, thinking about helping that couple.

She hadn't done much, really, just pointed out the obvious and made them see things a different way. Sometimes people needed that. And it had felt good to help someone, to be connected.

That was what she was missing in life. Since she'd retired, she had no purpose, no goals. She'd thought she'd be traveling with her husband, but he'd had other plans, and she'd done nothing to fill that void. She needed to settle down and get a job. Was Lobster Bay the place?

But how could she afford it? She didn't have very much in her 401k and couldn't withdraw it without a penalty anyway. She had a little bit in savings, but she was too young for Social Security and had no job. Maybe she could get a job at the school or the assisted living place where her father once was. Her education and experience would be useful for either. She'd get a third of the sale of this house, but after paying the realtor fees, back taxes, and other bills, that might not amount to enough for another place in town.

Her phone interrupted her train of thought. It was Sophie, her daughter, trying to FaceTime her.

"Mom! So sorry I haven't called. Luke has had the flu. I feel awful that you are out there doing all the work at Grampie's house and I can't come to help."

All her resentments about her kids not helping melted away. Naturally Sophie's first responsibility was to her two-year-old. And when she saw her daughter's anxious face and heard the sincerity in her voice, Liz knew that was all it was.

"I hope he's okay?" Now Liz was worried about her grandson.

Luke's cherubic two-year-old face appeared on the screen. "Gam!"

Liz's heart soared. He seemed fine. She certainly couldn't expect Sophie to get away with a little one at home. Liz remembered those times it was nearly impossible to get away. Sophie wouldn't be much help if she had to watch him, and even though Liz would love to visit, she had work to do.

"As you can see, he's fine. But, Mom, do you need help? I can have David take some time off work so I can come out."

"Oh no, I'm fine. Look!" Liz turned the camera around and panned the room so Sophie could see her handiwork.

"Wow, that looks nice. It's retro, and all of that is coming back in style. I think that place will sell in no time."

"You do?" Liz frowned. She didn't like the thought of it selling in "no time." But wasn't that what she wanted? Of course it was, because then she'd get her third of the sale and could use that money on another place. Strangely, though, she was slowly discovering she might not want *another* place.

CHAPTER TWENTY-THREE

The Arundel Armory was an old brick building with a creaky door that opened to a modest Civil War museum. Andie expected to find an old war veteran at the desk, but instead a young woman with heavy dark eyeliner, jet-black hair in a long ponytail, and an all-black outfit greeted her. Her name was Patty, according to the tag on her shirt.

"Hi. I was told you have Civil War archives with listings of the soldiers and their families."

Patty's dark brow quirked up, and she looked skeptical. "You want to dig around in there?"

Dig around? Andie was hoping for something with a computer screen. "I think so. I came across some discharge papers for a Civil War soldier and want to locate his descendants."

"Okee doke. The archives are over here."

Patty led her to a room in the back. It was chock-full

of old, dusty boxes with brittle yellowed papers. Andie was afraid to even touch any of them and aghast that they were kept in this condition.

"We're working on moving them to digital." Patty moved some of the papers from the top of a box, seemingly uninterested that the paperwork was disintegrating before her very eyes.

"I think you'd better hurry." Andie carefully opened a folder and took a piece of paper out, the edge crumbling beneath her fingers.

"They're more interested in the displays." Patty gestured toward the museum section with its tanks and guns and uniforms.

Voices emanated from the lobby, and Patty ran off to tend to them, leaving Andie with the archives. She studied the labels on the boxes, trying to figure out where to start. The boxes had a range of dates, so she started with the one that had the dates coinciding with the discharge papers.

Fortunately, the actual papers inside weren't as old as the mid-1800s. It looked like most of the information had been recorded or transcribed in the 1950s and filed in folders according to town. Sorting through the papers was tedious work, and after a few hours, she was about to give up when she finally found a lead on her guy.

She followed a paper trail for another hour. Apparently, Robert Koslachowski had been married and had one son. That son, Edward, had a son and daughter. The daughter had died before having any children, but the son had had two sons, and the last records of him were that they'd lived in the county. Unfortunately, that was where the family tree ended. There were no records of the two sons getting married, having children, or dying. At least not any that Andie could find.

Where did the two sons go? Andie made a mental note to check into the county records. The Civil War archives might not go that far, but surely the county would have some records. At least she knew that Robert had descendants, and, even though the trail ended, these records were old and incomplete. So it was back to the library with the new information to try to pick up the trail.

CHAPTER TWENTY-FOUR

Victoria Weathers showed up at Tides precisely on time for her interview. She was an older woman who wore a crisp white blouse and navy slacks. Her gray hair was cut short and fluffed on the sides. She had dark eyes that darted around, taking in every detail.

She'd accepted the offer of a cup of tea. Now she was perched on Grandma Miller's blue velvet wingback chair in the small sitting room on the south side of the inn, holding the dainty cup, pinkie extended.

Jane settled into the carved mahogany sofa across from her and looked over the woman's resume. At least hers had plenty of relevant experience. She didn't have any experience running a hotel, but Tides was a small operation, and the experience she did have as a housemother at a girls' school and as a nanny was along the same lines.

"So, Mrs. Weathers... or should I call you Victoria?" Jane smiled at the woman.

"Mrs. Weathers is fine. I think a level of formality is appropriate here, don't you?"

Jane's smile dimmed. This one seemed like a real fun person to have around. But Jane wouldn't be here when Mrs. Weathers was watching the inn, so maybe she should let that go. "Of course."

Mrs. Weathers gestured toward the resume. "As you can see, I have plenty of experience. I'm known for being responsible and prompt. You can call the references if you'd like."

"Great. So why did you leave your last job as..." Jane glanced down to the last job on the list. Nanny for the Rivers family in the next town over. "A nanny?"

"The children grew up. They were such lovely little cherubs. And so well-behaved. Mostly due to my influence, even if I do say so myself." Mrs. Weathers practically inflated with pride.

"I see. And why do you think working at Tides will be a good fit?"

"Well, it's part-time, which suits me, as I'm semi-retired." She glanced around the room as if taking inventory. "And I know how to take care of things and treat people."

"And you don't mind greeting them and answering phones?"

"Not at all. I'm very efficient and run a tight ship."

Her eyes fell on Cooper, who had trotted in and sat on the floor next to Jane. "Oh, you allow dogs?"

Jane's hand dropped to pat Cooper, who thumped his tail against the leg of the coffee table, apparently unaware of Mrs. Weathers's disapproval. "Guests love him."

Mrs. Weathers said nothing, but her brows rose a notch. "Oh, well, it seems a little... unsanitary." Her eyes fell on the cut glass candy dish loaded with chocolate kisses, and Jane felt more disapproval radiating from the woman.

"No one has complained about Cooper. People love the little candies we leave around, and sometimes we have cookies out in the foyer when guests are checking in." Jane was proud of the little extras they offered at Tides.

Mrs. Weathers shifted in her seat. "I see. All those hands touching the food seems a little risky, don't you think?"

"Risky?" Seemed like Mrs. Weathers was a germaphobe and maybe a little bit strict. Jane already thought she might not be a good fit.

"Germs. But I suppose people do like food. Speaking of which, your pamphlet says you provide lodging and breakfast. No other meals?" Mrs. Weathers took the Tides brochure out of her purse, as if she needed to remind Jane about her own pamphlet. Jane added "condescending" to her list of dislikes about the woman.

"Sometimes we have a light snack in the afternoon, and if there's a special event, we might offer a meal, depending on the event."

"And would I be expected to serve the guests?" Mrs. Weathers's facial expression suggested that she considered serving food a most unpleasant task.

"We usually do a buffet, and guests serve themselves, but sometimes Brenda—she's our cook—or I walk around to top off the coffees and make sure everything runs smoothly. I find it's nice to chat with the guests. Those personal touches make for good word of mouth about the place when people get back home."

Mrs. Weathers wore a look that indicated she was considering the matter. "I suppose it must. What time precisely do you put breakfast out?"

"Brenda usually gets the buffet loaded up around eight and keeps bringing dishes out as needed until ten." Jane was starting to feel like she was the one being interviewed for a job.

"What is the menu? Do you have a sample?" Mrs. Weathers glanced at the credenza that was set against the wall as if expecting to find menus there.

"We don't have a menu per se. We offer the basics that most people like and a bit of whatever Brenda feels like making."

"Sounds a bit unorganized." Mrs. Weathers pursed her lips. "So there are no other meals or duties? Laundry? Lugging bags upstairs? Cleaning?"

"We have a maid, people take their own bags up, and I use a laundry service, so none of that. Sometimes we might have an event that involves a small party or extra food."

"Yes, I've heard you do weddings. Would more be expected of me during those times?"

They'd had one wedding, but Jane had gotten a few queries for more next summer. "Not really. There might be a rush of people checking in the few days before the wedding, but I'd probably make sure either me or my sister, Andie, was on duty to help."

"Very good. Well, it is a lovely place you have, and the location can't be beat. It really is perfect for weddings, and the family heirlooms and antique furniture add a nice touch." Mrs. Weathers's compliment appeared genuine.

Jane smiled. Maybe Mrs. Weathers wasn't so bad after all.

They each asked a few more questions, and Mrs. Weathers was quite pleasant. As the interview drew to a close, however, Jane had the sinking feeling that she wasn't the right candidate. She wanted so badly to tell Mike that she'd hired someone before this situation caused a problem between them. As it was, she'd just had to turn down a lunch invitation from him. While he hadn't said anything about that, she'd sensed his frustration. She didn't want to ruin their relationship. He was important to her, but Tides was important too.

CHAPTER TWENTY-FIVE

Andie was fairly familiar with the neighborhood Liz Weston's house was in because one of her best friends in grade school had lived there. Stella Macintyre had moved away when they were in junior high, and Andie had lost touch years ago, but she recognized the house, even though the trees and shrubs had grown a lot since she'd last been there.

The street was quiet with mature landscaping. The homes were older ranches and split-levels that had been built around the 1970s on large lots. Some of them had been remodeled, and most had been kept up nicely. Except for the Weston home.

The one beside Liz's was cute as a button with a rose trellis out front and window boxes and... wait. Was that Maxi's car in the driveway?

As she squinted toward the car, Maxi came out of the house.

"Hey, fancy meeting you here," Andie said out the window as she parked in Liz's driveway.

"Andie?" Maxi hitched the straps of her tote bag back up her shoulder and came over to the car. "What are you doing here?"

"Remember our guest, Liz, who is in town to clean out her family home?"

"Yeah."

Andie pointed toward the house. "Well, that's her house. She asked me to come over and evaluate some of the old items she's found."

"Oh, right. Bunny did say she lived there."

"Who's Bunny? What are you doing here anyway?"

Maxi turned to look at the house she'd just come from, her expression a bit embarrassed. "Bunny is an artist, and I'm taking painting lessons, if you can believe that."

"For the pet portrait of Goblin?" Andie felt sympathetic and wanted to encourage her. "That's great. I'm sure it will help."

Maxi smiled. "Already is."

Liz had come out the front door with two large cardboard boxes brimming with items. She set it down beside two other equally full boxes and came to join Andie and Maxi. "Hey, Andie, glad you could stop by."

"I'm happy to." Andie turned to Maxi. "This is my friend Maxi."

"Nice to meet you. I was just over at Bunny's." Maxi's gaze fell on the box Liz had just put down. "That's a great lamp."

Liz turned to the box. "It is? I was going to throw it out. It was in the living room for ages." She looked back at Andie. "Maybe you should look through the boxes. I really have no idea what is valuable and what isn't."

Andie picked the lamp out of the box. It was tall with a bulbous base and long neck. The shade was a bit dirty and tattered, but the pink glass base was handblown. "This is actually a highly sought-after example of mid-century lighting. Worth a couple hundred."

"Oh!" Liz grimaced and looked back in the boxes. "Good thing you came before the trash guy."

Maxi had moved closer to the boxes and was poking around inside them. "You shouldn't throw some of this out. At least not yet. It would be perfect for staging the house."

"Staging?" Liz asked.

"Yeah, you're selling it, right?"

Liz nodded.

"Houses look better when they are set up as if people are living there except without the clutter," Maxi said.

"Maxi is a wiz at decorating. She decorated my apartment, and it looks like it could be in a magazine." Andie couldn't help but compliment her friend. The apartment really had come out amazing thanks to Maxi.

"Gosh, I don't know much about selling houses. I was just supposed to be cleaning it out before we put it on the market, but if it will sell better with the things still in it…"

"It will. I'd be happy to help you if you want," Maxi offered.

"Oh, I couldn't ask you to do that," Liz said. "I could talk to my brother and sister and see if they want to hire you."

"Nonsense." Maxi took Liz's arm and led her toward the front door. "Let's go see what we have to work with."

Inside, the house was like a time capsule. Andie was surprised to recognize things that reminded her of her own childhood.

"We had this same clock at our house!" Andie pointed at the starburst clock hanging over the fireplace.

"We did too. And I think we had that same coffee table with the slats in it." Maxi turned in a slow circle, taking it all in. "And the colors!"

"You like them?" Liz frowned as she looked at the avocado, gold, and green color scheme that permeated the house.

Maxi pursed her lips as she considered the question. "Well, it is very vintage."

"It hasn't changed much since I was little," Liz said.

"Maybe that's not very good for resale. Not everyone wants those colors. You should probably try to diffuse them with more neutral tones to appeal to a broader range of buyers." Maxi fluffed an orange-and-yellow pillow that sat on the green couch. "But something that goes with the color of the furniture and accessories, since you don't want to buy all new things. Maybe a light beige or gray?"

Liz looked skeptical. "I was actually going to have Goodwill come and take the furniture. Do you think I should leave it here?"

"Yes, of course! People need to be able to envision how they might live here." Maxi walked over to the large brick fireplace in between the living room and kitchen. "But get rid of anything personal and all the knickknacks on the mantel and side tables."

"I'll look over them and let you know which ones can be tossed and which have value," Andie volunteered.

Maxi picked up a picture of a smiling family and a dog that had been on the mantel. "I'm sure you'll want to keep some things for sentimental reasons. Is this your family?"

Liz stood next to Maxi, a smile spreading on her face as she pointed out the people in the picture. "That's Mom and Dad. My sister, Shelly, and brother, Peter. The goofy kid is me. And, of course, our family dog, Ranger."

"Looks like you were happy. Are your brother and sister coming to help you sort through the house?"

Liz looked a little sad, and Andie wondered why. Were the siblings leaving all the work to Liz? Then again, Liz was retired. Maybe they had an agreement.

"I'm not sure. They're very busy." Liz glanced around the room. "And I guess none of us really care much about sentimental things. At least I thought I didn't."

Andie could see the conflict on Liz's face and knew exactly how she felt. "You thought coming home would be depressing and stressful, but now that you're looking around, you're finding being home brings up comforting memories, too, aren't you?"

Liz looked surprised. "How do you know?"

"Same thing happened to me." Andie took a breath. She hadn't talked much about this, but it seemed important for Liz to know that you really could come home again. "I left Lobster Bay right after high school and avoided coming back. Bad memories were tied up in this town."

"I know what you mean. But somehow now the memories don't seem so bad. I think I was making too much of them when I was younger, and that just festered over the years," Liz said.

Andie nodded. "Same here. When my mother's health started to decline, I had to come back to help with the Inn. Funny thing, though, at first I thought it would only be temporary. I dreaded coming back and facing all those memories. But it turned out that coming home brought up comforting memories instead, and I decided to stay."

"You did? So you recently moved back here?" Liz asked.

"Yep."

"And do you regret it?"

"Not one bit." Andie glanced at Maxi. "The people here are great, and you can't beat being near the beach."

"You can say that again." Liz gestured toward the hallway. "There are a lot of things in the bedrooms, and now I have no idea which ones are worth money. Maybe we could have some coffee and a muffin, and then you could take a look?"

"I'd love to." Andie followed Liz to the kitchen. Liz

seemed a little happier since their conversation. If Andie wasn't mistaken, Liz was looking at her old childhood home with new eyes.

CHAPTER TWENTY-SIX

Liz was surprised at the amount of money Andie offered for the items she'd said were valuable. Andie had suggested that Liz could look them up online and see if she felt the offer was fair. Considering that Liz had thought most of the items were trash, she didn't see the need. She trusted Andie and was happy to get some extra money that she hadn't been counting on.

Should she have consulted her siblings? Maybe, but they hadn't expected to get any money, either, so Liz considered it a windfall and was happy to save the time. Peter hadn't been that concerned about it when she'd spoken to him, and she was sure Shelly felt the same. Plus, the extra money could pay for the new interior paint, which she needed to get done right away.

Andie had hauled most of the items away, leaving only a few pieces she would pick up later. Then she and Maxi had helped Liz lug the junk boxes to the curb.

Clearing out all of it made a huge difference. Maybe she should save the estate some money and move out of Tides. Giving up a free room at a quaint inn on the beach seemed crazy, but she felt at home here in the house now.

Don't get too comfortable. She was only here until the house got fixed up. Then it would be sold. And after that, she had nowhere to go until she got her portion of the house sale. Not knowing how much that would be was stressful. It surely wouldn't be enough to buy another place outright. Would a bank give her a loan if she had no income?

She didn't want to dwell on her current lack of opportunities. If worse came to worst, she could rent a small place somewhere. Rents were expensive these days, and it would be a drain on her savings, but if she went to a more rural town, she would find cheaper rents.

For now, she'd better call Shelly and update her on the progress.

"Liz, how is it going? Do you need anything?" Shelly sounded chipper, and Liz appreciated the offer.

"It's going good. I don't need anything. There's been a few developments."

"Oh?"

"It turns out some of the things Mom and Dad had are worth a little money, so I had an antique dealer come and look at them."

"Really? What was worth money?"

Liz hesitated. She hoped Shelly wouldn't be mad. What if she wanted to keep an item for sentimental reasons? But if that were the case, she should have said something or come here to secure it. "Things you would never think of. Salt and pepper shakers. Ashtrays. End tables."

"Wow. Who knew?"

"I hope you don't mind that I sold them. The place needs a fresh coat of paint, and I was going to use the money to pay for that. It will sell a lot better with new paint." At least Maxi thought so.

"I don't mind at all. You're in charge, so whatever you decide is good with me. Are you going to stay in the house now?"

"I'm not sure. I've made good headway cleaning it, and I know putting me up at Tides is expensive, but…"

"Look, don't worry about the money. If Dad's savings run out, I can chip in."

Liz didn't want Shelly to pay for her lodging. She felt guilty enough as it was that she was eating into what they would eventually divide among the three of them.

"I'd love to see what you've done with the place, and I wish I was there. There must be so many things from when we were kids. Did you find my Barbie dolls, by any chance? Those are probably worth money now."

Liz laughed. "I doubt it. Ranger chewed the feet, remember?"

"I thought that was you who chewed them," Shelly teased.

"Maybe. I think Mom got rid of our old toys when we

all went to college. I can take some pictures and send them. The place looks pretty good now."

They chatted for a few more minutes, and then Liz hung up and took some pictures with her smartphone and texted them to her sister.

She sent the text to Peter, too, and then called. They had a similar conversation about the state of the house and the items she'd sold. He claimed he was looking at his busy schedule and trying to clear it to come out and help. She wasn't holding her breath.

Next, she called Sally Littlefield. Maxi had given her the woman's name and said she'd be great for painting the walls. Sally seemed very nice. She could start right away and was willing to come over to give an estimate on the job in a few hours.

Liz picked some tomatoes from the garden and was washing them in the sink when a knock sounded on the front door. Was Sally here already? She opened the door to reveal a woman in her early fifties holding a casserole.

"Hi. I'm Sheila Donahue from number six." The woman turned to look at a gambrel down the street. The house was the same age as Liz's but had been much better cared for with a trim lawn, colorful flowers, and fresh paint. Sheila looked well cared for, too, with honey-blond hair and sharp blue eyes. She was wearing a flowered T-shirt and faded jeans. Liz liked her right away.

Liz introduced herself and reached out and took the casserole. "Nice to meet you. Won't you come in?"

They sat in the kitchen, and Liz dished out small

pieces of the chicken enchilada casserole. Sheila had even brought sour cream and guacamole. It was cheesy and delicious with just a hint of spice. Maybe it was a good thing she wasn't living here; with the way neighbors brought over food, she'd certainly gain some weight.

"I was hoping that you were moving in." Sheila had been disappointed when Liz explained that she was only cleaning out her father's house and that it would soon go up for sale. "Ever since the kids went to college, it's been kind of boring around here. I used to drive them to soccer and friends' houses, so now I have a lot of time on my hands. I could use someone my age to liven things up."

Liz liked the idea of that. She'd spent the last decade focusing on her kids and then, when they went out on their own, on her marriage. Fat lot of good that last part had done her. She didn't really have any close friends. For the rest of her life, she wanted to focus on herself and having good friends to spend the time with.

"It is a nice neighborhood. What about the other neighbors?" Liz asked. Even though Bunny had already given her the lowdown, she wanted Sheila's impression.

"Emma is such a darling, and her little daughter, Avery, is so cute."

Liz forked off a small bite from the casserole on her plate.

"I give her a lot of credit, raising that kid all on her own, and she's doing a great job. Her ex-husband is kind of a jerk."

"Aren't they all." Liz noticed Sheila's coffee mug was

empty. Had they been talking that long? She stood and pointed at the coffee pot. "More coffee?"

"That would be great." Sheila slid her mug across the table. "And Mrs. Svenson is very sweet. She's over ninety, you know. I could sure use some help with her. We try to help her in the yard, and I check on her quite frequently to make sure she hasn't fallen or anything." Sheila laughed. "It won't be long before someone's doing that for me!"

They talked their way through another cup of coffee. Liz wasn't surprised to discover that they had a lot in common. They discussed everything from their careers to their kids to the benefits of living in Lobster Bay.

When she finally showed Sheila out, Sally was pulling into the driveway in her work truck.

The handywoman wasn't anything Liz had expected. She must've been in her seventies but looked thin and spry. She had a long gray braid wound up around her head. Her face was tanned, and her blue eyes sparkled with intelligence.

"This looks like a fairly easy job," Sally said. "I'll have to measure the space to give you a quote."

"Of course. When do you think you could start?"

"You're in luck. Mrs. Oberman's granddaughter had her twins early, so she put off the work I was going to do on her sunroom next week. I could start right away."

Liz smiled. "That's perfect. Guess we better get measuring, then."

CHAPTER TWENTY-SEVEN

Jane felt bad about having to refuse Mike's invitation to lunch, so she baked his favorite chocolate chip banana bread and headed over to his place with Cooper.

Mike lived in a townhouse in a development called Boulder Hills. Even though Jane did have responsibilities at Tides, she was still able to carve out enough personal time to spend quite a bit of it at the townhouse. She felt right at home there, which she should have because Mike had consulted her on every aspect of its decor and even on which unit to buy. She wondered if maybe he was going to ask her to move in, but how could she do that? She needed to be at Tides to run it. It was too much to think about.

Cooper raced to the front door, and Jane rang the bell, feeling a little nervous. Mike had given her a key, but she didn't feel right walking in unless he knew she was coming. And considering how frustrated he'd sounded when she'd had to say no to lunch, she wasn't even sure if she'd be welcome.

He opened the door with a curious expression on his face. His brown curly hair was tousled, as if he'd been running his hands through it. His green eyes widened when he realized who was at the door.

"Jane! I wasn't expecting you. Thought you had an interview?" He bent and petted Cooper, who wriggled with excitement.

"I hope you don't mind me dropping by?" Jane hesitated.

"Of course not." He sounded sincere. She'd been worried he was mad about the lunch thing, but maybe that was just her overactive imagination.

She held up the tinfoil-wrapped loaf. "I made some banana bread as a peace offering for missing lunch."

Mike laughed and took the bread. "A peace offering is not necessary, but I'm not going to turn down fresh baked banana bread." He opened the door wider, and Cooper raced right in.

Jane followed him to the kitchen. She loved the white cabinets, the marble counters, and the breakfast nook with its large windows. She'd picked it all out, and Maxi had helped decorate it with splashes of sunny yellow and bright blue.

Mike got out a cutting board and cut two slices of bread while Cooper ran around sniffing every square inch, as if expecting the condo to be full of new smells since the last time he was there, just two days ago.

"How did the interview go?" Mike asked.

Jane settled into a chair at the breakfast bar on the other side of the counter from where Mike was working. "Not very good, I'm afraid. She insisted I call her *Mrs. Weathers*, and she seemed like a bossy fussbudget that would micromanage and disapprove of everything that went on at the inn."

Mike grabbed the butter tray out of the fridge. "So I guess she's out."

"Yeah, sorry."

He slid the plate of bread slices and butter over to her, and she picked up a piece.

"I'll try to get some better people in," she said. "I never realized how hard it would be to find somcone."

He sat beside her and gave her a kiss on the cheek. "Don't feel pressured. You need to find the exact right person, and if that takes some time, then so be it."

"But I thought you were getting frustrated with me because I had to spend so much time at the inn." Jane was a little relieved that maybe Mike was less put off than she'd thought.

Mike bit into his slice of banana bread and chewed for a bit before answering. "No. Not really. I mean, we have the rest of our lives to spend together."

Jane's heart hitched. Did he just say the rest of their lives?

He smiled and reached for another slice of bread.

"Besides, if breaking a lunch date means I get fresh baked bread, I won't mind if it happens a few more times."

CHAPTER TWENTY-EIGHT

Andie wrapped the antique porcelain pitcher carefully in tissue paper then placed it in a bag and handed it over to her customer. "This is going to look great in your china cabinet, Mrs. Litchfield."

"I think so, too, dear. Thank you."

Andie watched the elderly woman shuffle out of the shop, the bag clutched to her chest. Mrs. Litchfield was one of her best customers. She collected a special type of porcelain that was made in the Limoges area of France. The pitcher—hand-painted with cherubs and gold detail—was an excellent example and one of the nicest pieces Andie had seen in a while.

She picked up her feather duster and walked around the shop, swooshing the dust off the tops of the mahogany side tables and crystal candy jar lids. This was her favorite activity, walking around and looking at her inventory while the shop was quiet. The subtle creaking of the old floorboards and the smell of antique wood and lemon Pledge swirled in the air.

She opened the curio cabinet and gave the glass shelves a dusting. Her gaze fell on the box beside it that held the Civil War papers.

Her search of the county records for Robert Koslachowski's two great-grandsons hadn't yielded a thing. It was as if his family disappeared. Maybe they had, or maybe they had moved to another state. How many states should she check? Maybe checking just a few of the surrounding counties wouldn't take too long.

She settled in at the computer behind the counter and was so engrossed in her search that she didn't hear someone come in.

"Must be pretty interesting."

Andie jumped, dropping the notebook she'd been holding even though she hadn't found anything to take notes about.

Shane stood on the other side of the counter, looking amused. "What's so interesting?"

Andie sighed and stretched. "Sorry, I was looking up my Civil War guy."

"You still haven't found his family?"

"No. It's weird because I know he had two great-grandsons, but all traces seem to disappear." Andie had already filled him in on her visit to the armory.

"Oh. I'm sorry you're having a hard time. I know how important this is to you, but maybe there is no one to give the documents to. You've put a lot of work into this. Might be time to let it go."

The expression on his handsome face was sincere. She knew he had her best interests at heart. And maybe he was right. She was letting it take over too much of her life, and it was overshadowing the really important things—like Shane. She'd even considered skipping the morning coffee at Sandcastles the next day so she could do more research. But her sister Jane and her friends were too important to skip out on for this.

By getting those papers to the family, she would feel like she helped someone. But those people were strangers. Maybe she should focus on helping those closest to her instead.

Andie shut her laptop and stood. "You're right. Now, did you say you were going to take me to the beach so we could have a glass of wine and watch the sunset?"

CHAPTER TWENTY-NINE

Maxi had taken her latest painting home and set it on the easel next to the large picture window that overlooked the ocean. The cottage on the beach was her creative painting space, but she liked to take her finished work home to look at it in a different light.

James had a high-profile career at the bank, and they lived in an upscale home on the cliffs near the Marginal Way. Though she wasn't right on the ocean, her view was outstanding. Sometimes she could even hear the waves crashing on the rocks from her deck on the side of the house.

Maxi stood back and admired the painting. Bunny was a good teacher, and her rendition of the cats had improved. In this painting, the two cats were curled up on a blue velvet pillow. She was especially proud of the area where their fur met. It had been difficult to show the individual black and white hairs overlapping without creating a big mess.

Their eyes looked luminescent and alive with just the right amount of mischief. They looked so sweet and innocent relaxing on their cushion. Nothing like the mischievous rascals they were being right now as they ran around the living room, batting a toy and clawing the rugs.

James came down the stairs. "That looks great. Is that today's work?"

"Yes. I think my skills are improving."

"I agree."

A tinfoil ball skidded past them with Picasso right behind it. James intercepted him by picking him up and cradling him like a baby. Picasso let James cuddle him for about three seconds before trying to climb up onto James's shoulder. It was a new trick James was attempting to teach the cats so that they would perch on his shoulder like parrots. Picasso got on his shoulder but only for a second before leaping off to the floor. He landed gracefully on all four paws with only a soft thud.

"It makes me so nervous when they jump that far! I always think they're going to break a leg," Maxi said.

"They're made for it." James turned his attention back to the painting. "So, do you feel satisfied with the progress you're making and the lessons you took with Bunny Howard?"

"The lessons are great, and Bunny is nice." Maxi tilted her head to see the painting from a different angle. "I guess it is an improvement, but it's still not quite there yet."

"Don't worry, you'll get there. Why don't you take a break?"

It wasn't a bad idea, and she was getting kind of hungry. Her stomach grumbled, and James looked down at it. "Seems like you need one. I have steaks ready to go on the grill and a salad in the fridge."

"You do?" Was it dinnertime? Maxi had been so intent on the painting she'd lost track of time.

"I know it's a little early, but I figured we could eat an early supper and snuggle up by the fire pit. We don't have too many nights left to eat outside."

They'd installed a large gas fire pit on the patio earlier in the summer so they could extend their outdoor season.

"Sounds like a good plan. I just need to get out of my painting clothes."

Maxi ran upstairs and changed into her comfortable jeans and a pink sweatshirt with Lobster Bay written in white on the front. She grabbed a soft, thick, knee-length gray sweater from the closet and joined James on the patio. The sizzle of steaks and the smell of grilling meat made her mouth water. James had set plates out on the edge of the fire pit, which was wide enough to use as a table. A bowl of salad sat on the side table in between two cushioned patio chairs.

"It doesn't get much better than this," Maxi said. "Can I help with something?"

"I have this under control. Maybe you could get that bottle of wine and a couple of glasses."

Maxi returned with the wine just as the steaks were coming off the grill.

They relaxed into their chairs around the fire pit. The steaks were grilled to a perfect medium rare with a little bit of char on the ends, just the way Maxi liked them. Her mouth watered as she cut off a piece.

"So, how was work today?" she asked James. Lately, their conversations had focused on her painting issues, and she didn't want everything they talked about to be about her.

"Pretty good. Nothing too exciting ever happens at the bank."

Maxi laughed. "Well, sometimes that's good."

"What did you do today? I hope you didn't spend the whole day hunched over your easel at the cottage."

Maxi told him about how she'd run into Liz and Andie. "The house is like a time capsule. I gave her some advice on staging the house."

"Another thing that you're excellent at." James looked over at their house. "Our place could be in magazines thanks to all the great work you've done decorating it."

Maxi had enjoyed decorating the house. The kitchen was a gorgeous light-gray with wide pine flooring and white quartz counters. The living room was white with blue and yellow accents. Their bedroom, in blues and yellows, was soothing. Maybe she should consider redoing the master bath, which hadn't been redone since before she had the kids.

"I ran into Marie Lapino at the bank today. She was really grateful for the donations we've been collecting in the lobby."

Marie ran the Lobster Bay animal shelter. Since bringing Picasso and Rembrandt home, James and Maxi had become somewhat active in trying to help her cause. The shelter always needed things like blankets, crates, food, and cleaning products. Maxi liked to scour yard sales for soft toys and cheap animal accessories and always bought pet food when it was on sale at the grocery store.

"That reminds me, I have a pile of stuff cluttering up the hall closet. I'll bring that down to her tomorrow."

"Good idea. It won't be long before we are using the closet for our fall jackets." James's lips quirked in a teasing smile. "Just be careful you don't come home with another cat."

CHAPTER THIRTY

Liz watched Sally Littlefield as she measured the wall surfaces to determine the scope of the project. The older woman sure was a character. Liz liked her no-nonsense attitude and could tell she was a hard worker.

"Looks like about a three-day job." Sally stood back and looked up at the ceiling. "Unless you want the ceiling done too."

Liz glanced up. The ceiling did look a bit yellowed, and as far as she could remember, her parents never had it painted. "I probably should. How much time will that add?"

"Just a day." Sally pulled a pencil from behind her ear and a piece of paper from her back pocket. She licked the end of the pencil and started scribbling then held the piece of paper out to Liz. "Here's the estimate."

It looked reasonable and wouldn't even use all the

money she'd gotten from Andie for the antiques. "Sounds good."

"What about the other rooms? As I recall, there are three bedrooms and the kitchen. Kitchens usually need ceiling paint."

"As you recall? You've been here?"

"Ayuh. Knew your mom—she was a peach. Then played poker with your dad and the gang in later years."

The gang? It seemed funny to think of her dad having a gang of poker-playing friends.

"He was a peach too. I was really sorry to hear of his passing."

"He was a peach? Never heard him described that way."

Sally laughed. "He was always talking about you kids."

"Really?"

"Ayuh. He was especially proud of you and your good grades. Said he always knew you could get into the best college with those grades, and that would be the best thing for your future."

Liz frowned. "Are you sure? As I recall, my grades were never good enough. He was always getting on me about them. Seemed to disapprove of everything I did."

Sally studied her for a few beats. "I think you might be remembering it from a teenager's perspective. When you're a teen you think you are invincible, and thinking about your future involves worrying what to wear to the next party. From an adult perspective, things look a lot different. Adults know how hard life is when you are on your own and how important it is to get a good start. Some fathers think they have to be tough to push their kids to do their best."

Had Liz done that with her own kids? There were plenty of times she had to be a lot sterner than she'd wanted. At least she'd had a soft side and hadn't been as bad as her father.

"You should have seen how my father treated me." Sally snorted. "But our parents were from a different generation. Their parents gave them tough love, and that's what they passed on. Didn't mean they didn't love us."

Liz looked around the room as Sally's words sank in. More memories surfaced, this time the bad ones, but now she saw them in a different light. She could see herself storming out the front door after one of the many fights. But hadn't her dad been calling after her to come back? And hadn't he treated her to ice cream or something special after? And the sofa where her father had waited up when she'd came in late… she'd assumed it was so he could catch her and yell at her for staying out past the time she was supposed to be home, but was it really because he was worried and couldn't sleep until she was home safe?

The way he'd kept on her about her grades… She'd seen it as not being good enough, but did he really want her to just do her best so she could have the best opportunities in life?

Could it be that she'd had everything wrong all along?

The house took on a whole new feeling. The new paint to match her new perspective would make it seem like it was her own. A new start with the best opportunities for a good future. Maybe it wouldn't be so bad to stay here until the house sold.

But the house was full of drop cloths and paint fumes, so it looked like she'd be staying at Tides a few more nights.

CHAPTER THIRTY-ONE

The next morning, Jane went to Sandcastles early. She sat at the table she and her friends favored. Cooper lounged on the warm sidewalk next to her. Hailey brought a mug of coffee, and Jane spread the classifieds out on the table. Since her visit with Mike, she was more determined than ever to find someone. Liz had been right. Jane might have been subconsciously tying herself to Tides to avoid taking that next step in her relationship. She needed to get over her fear and move on. She wanted to spend more time with Mike and see where that led.

The appearance of a plate of pastries on the table diverted her attention from the help wanted section she was studying. Claire slipped into the seat next to her, a mug of coffee in her hand.

"You looking for a job?" Claire joked.

Jane sighed. "Just studying the ads. Mine just doesn't seem to be working. No one new has applied."

"I thought you were interviewing someone yesterday?"

"Yeah, that didn't pan out." Was she being too critical? She hadn't called Mrs. Weathers yet to tell her she wasn't hired. Maybe she should give her a try. She might be better than nothing.

"Oh, sorry." Claire sipped her coffee, and Jane reached over to cut a bran muffin in half.

"It's not as easy as I thought it would be."

"Don't worry. Things will work out." Claire's gaze skipped over Jane's shoulder, and her brows pulled together. "Hey, is that Liz Weston? That woman looks familiar, and I know you said she was staying at Tides."

Jane twisted in her seat to see Liz walking down the sidewalk on the opposite side of the street. She waved at her. "Hey Liz!"

Liz looked up, a little confused at who would be calling her name. Then, upon recognizing Jane waving at her, she smiled and started over.

"I'm not sure if you guys know each other?" Jane gestured between Claire and Liz.

"I don't know." Liz squinted at Claire. "Hard to remember everyone from our younger days."

"Liz, meet Claire. She owns Sandcastles Bakery here. I highly recommend it! Would you like to join us?"

Liz hesitated, and Claire jumped up from her seat.

"Please do. I'll pull another chair over and get you a cup of coffee."

"Well, okay. Don't go to any trouble for me." But it was too late. Claire had already pulled a chair next to Jane and was halfway to the bakery door. Liz sat down and bent to pet Cooper.

"It's lovely here. Do they have good coffee?" Liz asked.

"The best." Jane took a sip of hers.

Claire returned with more pastries and a mug and small plate for Liz. "Help yourself."

"Just coffee for me." Liz patted her stomach. "I just had one of Brenda's delicious breakfasts at Tides with the nice couple that's staying there. The Silvermans."

"Those sure can fill you up," Claire said.

"How is the house cleanup coming along?" Jane asked.

"Pretty good. Andie came over and bought some of the old junk… er, I mean antiques," Liz joked. "And your friend Maxi gave me some pointers for staging and suggested I do some interior painting, so I hired this nice older lady, Sally, and she's starting today."

"Sally Littlefield?" Claire asked as she placed a steaming mug in front of Liz.

"Yes, that's her."

"She's great. Did a lot of work here." Claire gestured toward the bakery.

"And at Tides," Jane added.

"She seems very efficient. She said it would take three

days, so I'll be staying at Tides for a few more days at least."

"At least?" Jane raised her brows. "Does that mean you're thinking of moving into your old house?"

Liz shrugged. "Maybe."

"But you're still selling?" Claire asked.

"Probably." Liz sipped her coffee. "This is good."

"Are you having second thoughts about selling?" Jane asked.

Liz sighed. "It just seems so comfortable and familiar now, and my apartment is being turned into high-end condos, so I'm looking for a place—"

"Morning!" Andie plopped into a chair. "Hey, Liz, good to see you."

"You too. Thanks again for coming over to look at the things from my house," Liz said. "The money you gave me paid for the painting."

"I was happy to. It's what I do. I get inventory to sell, a collector gets something they really want, and you get money for something you no longer want. It's a win-win-win." Andie pinched a corner off a corn muffin and popped it in her mouth. "How did it go with Sally?"

"Great. She's hired."

"Oh, really? Gosh I'd love to see the place once she's done," Andie said.

"You would? Bunny mentioned that too. Maybe I'll have a little party to show it off."

"I bet Maxi would like that too." Andie frowned at

something across the road. "Hey, isn't that her over there?"

They turned to see Maxi heading down the sidewalk on the opposite side of the street. She waved at them and yelled. "I'll be there in a few minutes!" Then she headed straight on.

"Huh, that's weird." Claire cut a cheese danish in half and slid one half onto her plate. "I wonder where she's off to."

CHAPTER THIRTY-TWO

Maxi hoped the others didn't think she was avoiding them. She wasn't—well, not exactly. She had to drop stuff off at the animal shelter, and she had to admit that she hoped Bert and Harry would have finished their morning coffee and moved on by the time she was back. Although she was making progress on the painting of Goblin, she couldn't bear their hopeful looks and didn't want to make excuses again.

She pushed her doubts about the painting from her mind and focused on the joy of seeing all the animals at the shelter. Even though they were in between homes, the animals were always very happy, and the place was spotless. She definitely wasn't bringing home another cat, though. But there was no harm in looking at them.

She stopped in front of a cage containing a huge, fluffy striped cat with big yellow eyes. The tag said his name was Norse.

"Hey there." She poked her fingers through the cage, and the cat pressed his head against them. She scratched him, eliciting a low purr.

The cat in the next cage must have been envious. A dainty pink nose poked out of the cage, and the gray-and-white cat meowed loudly. Maxi moved over to give him attention.

"Maxi! Are you looking for another cat already?" Marie Lapino appeared from the back room with a mop in one hand and a sparkle in her eyes.

Maxi laughed. "I think the two I have are enough for now. I've been collecting towels and leashes from various yard sales and buying pet food when it's on sale. I wanted to drop it all off."

"Thank you so much." Marie leaned the mop against the wall and took the two large bags Maxi had brought. She peered in. "This is wonderful. I really appreciate it."

"I'm happy to do it."

"So, how are Rembrandt and Picasso doing?"

Maxi moved on to the next cat. She had a gorgeous charcoal-gray coat and blue eyes. "I think they're finally out of the terrible kitten stage. Some of my furniture didn't survive."

Marie laughed. "Kittens are rambunctious. Next time you could consider an older cat if you want to add to your family."

Another cat? Maxi wasn't ready for that yet. Maybe someday. Or if one caught her eye… Glancing around, she saw that almost all the cages were full. There were all kinds of cats with different colorings and markings. Most of them looked at her with curiosity in their eyes. She found herself thinking about how she would paint those eyes using the techniques she'd learned from Bunny. When she noticed the way the light reflected off them, she thought about where she would put the shadows and highlights and considered all the colors she would have to blend to get them just right. "You're pretty full up right now."

"We took some overflow from a shelter in Biddeford. Don't worry. They never stay long. All these little guys will get a forever home soon." Marie poked two fingers into a cage and petted a petite little calico. The cat rubbed her cheeks against Marie's fingertips. "Got a lot of dogs too. Maybe you need to adopt a dog to balance things out."

"Nice try. I don't think so, but I wouldn't mind saying hi to them."

"If you want to help me bring this stuff out back, you can check them out."

Maxi agreed, and they went back to the dog section. There was a German shepherd mix, a bulldog, a hound, and a little pug-terrier mix. The pug mix made her think of Bert and Harry. Were they ready for another dog? Maybe she should mention it to them.

She bent down in front of the bulldog's cage. The plate on the door said the dog's name was Shania. Her big brown eyes looked up at Maxi as if pleading for a home.

"Hey, Shania, you sure are pretty." Maxi turned to

Marie, who had squatted down beside her. "It's funny—their expressions seem human. And very different from cats. Cats seem to want to be waited on while dogs just want to be loved. You can see it in their eyes."

"Yep." Marie opened the door, and Shania stepped out so Maxi could pet her properly. "Cats' eyes are a different shape. Light hits them differently, and it makes them appear deeper but also without emotion. That's why their eyes seem so luminescent, almost glowing. It helps them see at night. Dogs' eyes just seem to go right to their souls."

Maxi stared at Marie. She was right! Could that be why her paintings of the cats were good while she was still struggling to paint Goblin? Could the answer be as simple as just adjusting the shape and reflection of the light?

Suddenly, she couldn't wait to get home and work on her painting, but first she had to meet her friends at Sandcastles.

CHAPTER THIRTY-THREE

Liz had just finished cleaning out the old bookshelf next to the fireplace, and Sally had just finished painting the living room when the doorbell rang.

A young woman in her mid-thirties stood on the doorstep. She was dressed in a tan T-shirt with crochet detail and striped linen pants. Comfy but not too casual. Her straight blond hair hung just below her shoulders, and she had wide-set blue eyes that brimmed with energy. She was holding a tray of sandwiches and a pitcher of lemonade. Boy, this neighborhood sure was big on bringing food.

"Hi! I'm Emma Chamberlain from number nine. Bunny said you're re-doing the house, and I saw you here working and thought you might need a break." Her eyes widened as she peered past Liz's shoulder into the living room. "Wow, this place looks great!"

"Thanks. I've cleaned a lot of my parents' stuff out, and I'm having it painted." Liz pointed at Sally.

"Hey, Sally." Apparently, everyone in town knew Sally, including Emma.

"Emma, how's the deck holding?"

"Great." Emma turned to Liz. "Sally fixed the deck on my house last year. She's the best."

"Come on in." Liz shooed her all the way in and shut the door. "How long have you lived in the neighborhood?"

"Just about eight years. I moved here with my daughter after the divorce."

"Did you know my dad?"

Emma nodded. "He was so nice to Avery. That's my daughter. She's in school right now. She was just little when he was here, but she used to come over when he was outside tending to the yard, and your dad would be so patient with her, explaining all about plants. I guess she needed a father figure."

Would the surprises never end? Liz was learning more and more about her dad.

"Anyway, I was so sorry to hear that he passed. We used to visit him up at Tall Pines."

"That was nice of you." Liz felt new guilt that Emma had probably visited her father more than she had. "Let's go eat in the kitchen. I'm starved. What about you, Sally?"

Sally eyed the platter as if she wasn't sure if she was invited.

"I made enough for all of us." Emma said.

"Well, I am pretty hungry."

"We both deserve a break." Liz herded Sally and Emma toward the kitchen. She paused at the doorway and looked back at the living room. All the clutter was gone, and the walls looked fresh and crisp with their coat of warm gray paint. "You did an awesome job."

"Thanks." Sally smiled with pride.

Liz got out plates and glasses, and everyone sat at the table.

"This house really looks good. I hope whoever you sell it to appreciates your hard work and is a nice neighbor." Emma took a bite of her sandwich. She'd brought an assortment—ham and swiss, tuna and egg salad, all cut into neat triangles.

Liz picked an egg salad triangle off the tray. The thought of someone else living in her house was unsettling. Especially since she'd just put so much work into it.

"Seems a shame to move out of this nice place," Sally said, as if reading her mind.

Liz looked around at the familiar, homey kitchen. Okay, maybe it could use new cabinets and granite counters, but it still felt comfortable and familiar.

"Why don't you just stay here?" Emma asked.

"I own it with my siblings, so we have to sell and split the money."

Emma nodded. "Of course, and I suppose you have your own home somewhere too."

"Actually, I don't. I moved into an apartment after my

divorce, and they're turning it into condos that I can't afford."

Emma nodded in sympathy. "I had a similar experience after my divorce."

"You might be able to afford it once this place sells." Sally crunched a chip. "You'll get one-third of the selling price. Unless there's a mortgage that could be a lot of money."

Liz frowned. Silly as it sounded, she actually hadn't considered that she could buy her old apartment. The mortgage had been paid years ago, but she had no idea what her third of the house sale would be. The house still needed work, and she wasn't sure how much they could sell it for. But did she even want to buy her old place? That seemed like a closed chapter in her life. She needed to open a new one.

"That's right," Emma said. "You can live in lots of places... maybe even here."

"Here?"

"Sure, you'd have enough for a down payment, or maybe you could work a deal with your siblings and not even have to get a loan." Sally chomped on her sandwich. "My friend Elsie's granddaughter did that after Elsie passed. She worked out some deal with her cousins and ended up with the house."

"It would be really great if you could stay," Emma said. "Bunny said you're just the right type for our little neighborhood."

But Liz was hardly listening. She was too busy

wondering if it was even remotely possible for her to work out a deal with her brother and sister. And if it was, how exactly would she go about that?

❦

After they finished up Emma's delicious sandwiches and Sally called it quits for the day, Liz called the investment broker with whom she had her retirement savings. She wanted to see if she could possibly use the leverage of her share of the property and her own retirement savings to take out some sort of a loan to pay her brother and sister.

He mentioned some possibilities, including taking out a loan against her retirement savings to pay them. He also asked some questions that she didn't know the answers to. What was the house worth? Would her siblings want a lump sum right away, or would they be willing to take payments?

But even if she could get some sort of loan like that, how would she make the payments? And there would be other household expenses, not to mention the property taxes. Without a big mortgage, all of that would be minimal, but she'd still need to supplement her income with a job. She had only a limited amount of savings to last her until she could collect Social Security and start tapping into her 401k.

But, at least, a plan was forming, and she felt more hopeful for the future than she had in a long time.

Would her siblings agree? There was only one way to

find out. She never asked for favors for herself, but the way Sally had put it, it didn't seem like it would be too much of a favor to let her use her portion for a down payment.

Brimming with determination to make her plan work, she called her sister.

"Liz! How's it going?" Shelly sounded a bit distracted. Liz hoped this wasn't a bad time because she wanted an answer right away.

"You won't believe it. The house looks so nice... almost too nice."

There was a beat of silence on the end of the line. "Huh? Too nice? Is that a problem?"

"Well, I had an idea, and I thought maybe—"

"Hold on, sorry..." Liz heard muffled sounds, as if Shelly had put the phone aside and was talking to someone else. Then Shelly came back on the line. "I'm sorry, Liz. I'm going to have to call you back later."

"But I just had this one thing, really quick—"

It was too late. Shelly had already hung up.

Maybe Liz would have better luck with her brother.

She made a cup of tea and then called Peter.

"Liz. Hi." Peter sounded very hesitant and guarded, which was odd. He was usually happy to hear from her.

"Hi, Peter. I'm just calling to update you on the house. I've cleaned out most of it and gotten it painted. It looks fantastic."

"That's great. I appreciate you doing all this work. Okay, well... gotta run."

"Wait a minute!" Why was Peter acting so weird? He usually chatted more. "I actually have an idea for the house, and I wanted to feel you out about it."

"An idea? Whatever you want to do, it is fine. You're doing a great job fixing it up. You can tell me about it later. I have an important—"

So Peter was going to brush her off too? Liz was sick of it, so she interrupted him. "No, Peter, really. I want to talk to you about this right now."

"I'm so sorry. I'm being called into a meeting." Peter hung up.

Liz stared at the phone. That was weird. Her siblings seemed to be purposely putting her off. Had they guessed what she wanted to ask and didn't know how to tell her no?

She felt angry. All her life she'd done things for them. And she'd come out here and done all this work on her own without them even lifting a finger. Granted, she had volunteered, and she had refused their offers to help, but still.... And now she wanted one little favor, and they couldn't even listen to her?

They both had plenty of money and didn't need the profits from the house right now, so they should have no reason to oppose the plan.

And her agent had said that after a few years, she could take out a home equity loan and pay them the rest. Couldn't they wait a few years for the money to make their sister happy?

Maybe she wasn't being fair. They couldn't have any

idea what she was about to propose. And she'd never told them the full truth about her situation because she didn't want them to feel sorry for her. They had no idea that she had no place to live. Maybe they both really *had* been busy, and Liz was reading too much into this.

Liz wandered around the house. The kitchen with its familiar layout was outdated, but, in time, she could renovate it and make it her own. The living room where they'd had family game nights looked retro modern with the fresh coat of paint. The old wall-to-wall rug would have to go, but Liz was pretty sure there were hardwood floors underneath it.

Her old bedroom would be a perfect office. Shelly's would make a nice guest room, and Peter's could be used for storage. The spacious master with its en suite bathroom would be a perfect bedroom for her. She could already picture it painted a calming light blue. Maybe she should add that to Sally's list.

Suddenly she was more determined than ever to stay in Lobster Bay and in this very house. No matter what the obstacles were, she was going to overcome them.

CHAPTER THIRTY-FOUR

A young woman was coming out of Tides when Andie arrived for her afternoon shift.

"Good afternoon!" Andie chirped.

"Afternoon." The woman mumbled, keeping her head down and shuffling away as if afraid.

Jane was standing in the lobby with a clipboard in her hand.

"Who was that?" Andie gestured toward the door.

"Latest interviewee."

"Not a keeper?" Andie said as Jane ripped the paper off the clipboard and tossed it in the trash.

"Afraid not." Jane motioned for Andie to follow her into the sitting room. "Did you see her? She was definitely not the outgoing type. We need someone who would be personable with the guests."

"That's too bad. How many people are you going to have to interview before you find the right one?" Andie asked. Just like Shane had suggested last night, she should be spending less time looking for her Civil War solider's family and more time helping her sister. She didn't even know if there were any Koslachowskis left or it they would even care about the papers of some long-forgotten relative. "I should be helping you with the interviews."

Jane waved her off. "Don't worry about it. You have the antique business to run. I just have Tides."

"But still." A pinch of guilt made Andie decide that if a new application came in, she would offer to interview the next person.

Jane took the couch, and Andie flopped into the chair. Cooper trotted over to lie in the puddle of sun coming in from the picture window. Jane frowned at Andie. "You seem a little down. Is something wrong?"

Andie reached over and plucked a chocolate kiss out of the dish. "Not really." She unwrapped the kiss and popped it into her mouth.

Jane took her own chocolate kiss out and started to unwrap it. "Seriously. What's wrong?"

Andie felt silly. Her problem with the Civil War document was nothing compared to other people's problems. On the other hand, she was grateful her sister cared. For many years, Jane and Andie had been estranged. Now that she'd moved back to town, they enjoyed a close relationship, and she wanted to keep it that way. That meant telling her everything, no matter how silly it seemed. "It's just the Civil War document. I've run into a dead end trying to find the family."

"Oh, that's too bad. That seems like something a family would want. So what are you going to do? Are you just giving up?"

Andie picked another kiss out of the bowl. Jane did the same.

Andie rolled the velvety chocolate around in her mouth slowly as she thought about what she was going to do. "I think so. I might've been getting a little obsessed about it."

They plucked two more kisses out of the bowl and unwrapped them.

"So what will you do with the document?" Jane asked as she popped her kiss into her mouth.

"Not sure. It doesn't feel right to sell it. Maybe I'll just save it in case someone comes looking."

"That sounds like a good idea." Jane plucked another kiss out of the bowl.

"What about you? Is it causing problems with Mike that you haven't found someone to take more shifts at Tides? I could add a few to my schedule." Andie leaned forward and took another kiss from the bowl.

"Don't worry about it. I thought he was upset that I couldn't go to lunch the other day, but then I bribed him with some fresh banana bread, and everything seems to be okay."

Andie laughed. Scooping a handful of the kisses out of the dish, she settled back into her chair. "Well, that's good. You guys make a nice couple."

Jane smiled, her cheeks turning the slightest shade of pink. "We do, don't we?"

The two sisters chatted about some ideas for bringing more guests to Tides. They exchanged town gossip and wondered how their mother was getting along at the assisted living facility.

Suddenly, Andie looked at the bowl. "Oh my gosh, we ate this whole bowl of chocolate kisses!"

Jane looked at the pile of silver foil wrappings in front of her. "Geez, I guess I wasn't paying attention. Guess I'll have to have salad for supper."

Andie laughed. "Yeah, me too. Seems like I just look at food and the pounds go on."

"Don't I know it."

"You're not the only ones," Liz Weston said from the doorway. "Sorry, I couldn't help but overhear about the pounds going on."

Cooper trotted over to her, wagging his tail rapidly as she stooped to pet him.

"Come on in and join us." Jane gestured toward the empty chair. "Sorry there's no more chocolate."

"I'm on my way to my room, but I was looking for you two so I could invite you to a little reveal party I'm having to show off the house. It's mostly cleaned out now, and Sally is almost done with the painting."

"How does it look?" Jane asked.

"Fabulous. I can't believe the difference."

"I'm dying to see it," Andie said.

"Great. Sally is coming, and so are Bunny Howard

and a few of the other neighbors. Could you invite Maxi and that nice lady from the bakery?"

"Claire?" Jane asked.

"Yes. She was so gracious to me the other morning."

"Of course. She'd love to come, and Maxi will be excited to see the change."

"Great." Liz bent down and petted Cooper again. "And you're invited, too, Cooper. Tomorrow night at six o'clock."

CHAPTER THIRTY-FIVE

Maxi stood back and assessed the painting. Her back hurt from standing at the easel for almost eight hours, and she had paint all over her clothes and hair. But the ocean breeze billowing the curtains beside the open French doors and the sound of waves crashing on the beach made up for it.

This was her best attempt yet. She was getting close but...

Knock, knock.

She leaned out to look through the kitchen and saw Claire peering in the door. She was holding a basket and looked concerned.

Maxi put the brush in turpentine and turned her painting to face the wall. She wasn't ready for anyone to see it.

"You haven't been answering your phone," Claire said.

"Sorry, I got carried away painting." Maxi was touched by her friend's concern.

"James came into Sandcastles for a coffee and said you were here painting. He hadn't heard from you, either, and suggested you might need a snack." Claire put the basket down on the kitchen table and pulled the red gingham towel off the top.

Bakery smells wafted out, and Maxi realized she was, indeed, ravenous. Inside the basket was an assortment of muffins, cookies, and brownies. Maxi picked out a corn muffin, put on some coffee, and set some mugs and dessert plates on the Formica table.

"Want to go sit out on the patio?"

Maxi had rented the cottage furnished, but she'd brought over a lot of furniture and accents to make it her own. Her favorite was the patio set that she'd put out back. The cottage had a small area with pavers that sat right on the beach, and she loved to sit out there. Sometimes in the summer, she and James got up early and came from their house on the cliff to watch the sun rise before he headed off to work and she started painting. But it was gorgeous to sit out any time of day. Now, in the late afternoon, it was still warm enough if you wore a sweater.

They sat out watching a few beachgoers stroll through the waves at the edge of the ocean. It was low tide, and the edge of the waves was a good three hundred feet away. Just far enough to keep the patio private but still be able to see the waves.

"This is great. Thanks. I didn't realize how hungry I was." Maxi cut the muffin in half and spread butter on it.

"There's another reason I was calling." Claire dunked a cookie into her coffee.

Maxi looked up from her muffin. "Oh?"

"Yes. We got invited to a little party at Liz Weston's. She's done with sprucing the house up and wanted to show it off."

"That's great! That house is so cute. I can't wait to see what she's done. Who is going?"

Claire squinted as if to remember. "You, me, Jane, Andie, and I think they said she had asked some neighbors."

"Probably Bunny Howard. I took a painting lesson with her." Speaking of painting, Maxi really wanted to focus on finishing the painting of Goblin for Bert and Harry. Her eyes strayed over to the window, where she could see the easel facing the wall. She had just a few things to try… but taking a break would be good. Besides, she needed to let some of the underlayers dry before putting in the details that she hoped would pull it all together.

Maybe her subconscious would fill in the blanks to the last piece she was missing. Besides, she would never turn down an opportunity to hang out with her friends. "When is the party?"

"Tomorrow night at six."

"Sounds good. Is Rob going? Do you want to go together?"

"Rob isn't going. It seems like it's just a quick reveal, and he didn't seem interested. I'd love to go together. I can pick you up."

A noise at the window caught their attention. They looked over to see Rembrandt pressing his face against the window. His mouth opened in a meow, and he glared at them.

"He wants to go out," Maxi said.

"I get that look from Urchin too." Claire's gray cat, Urchin, was a favorite of Maxi's, and she always looked forward to visiting Claire's little cottage so she could see him. She especially anticipated those visits before she'd adopted two cats of her own.

"It's too dangerous to let them out alone. I can only imagine the trouble they would get into," Maxi said. "You'd think they'd get enough with traveling from our house to the cottage and back again every day."

"Cats are never satisfied," Claire said.

"You can say that again." Maxi settled back in her chair, her hand wrapped around the warm mug. "So, what have you been up to?"

"Not much. Still gathering recipes for fall." Claire snugged her aqua hoodie with the Sandcastles bakery logo on it a little tighter. "Rob has the pumpkin bread market cornered, but I figured I could do the usual pumpkin cream cheese muffins. I also want to try something different, though."

"Like what?" Just the mention of Claire's pumpkin

cream cheese muffins had Maxi's mouth watering, even though she'd already gobbled down her corn muffin.

"I'm not really sure. Maybe something like pumpkin spice cream horns or sweet potato danish."

"Hmm..." Maxi took a sip of coffee. Neither of those sounded particularly appetizing, but she didn't want to say that to Claire.

"Jane was thinking of having an event at the inn for Oktoberfest to bring more people there, and I was thinking I could whip up something really unusual that she could offer them."

Jane liked to order desserts from Claire's bakery and breads from Rob's bread store to serve to guests at the inn. It was one of the nice ways that people in Lobster Bay worked together.

Thoughts of October made Maxi frown. It was still a ways off, but she didn't relish the colder temperatures or the leaves falling from the trees. But those bleak late fall days would turn to winter soon enough, and she'd be cozied up in front of her fireplace while the snow fell outside and her Christmas tree twinkled in the corner. That was something she could look forward to.

"I hope Jane finds some help at the inn before then. She works too much," Maxi said.

"She needs to slow down. Maybe we all do," Claire said, shrugging. "But I love work, and Jane probably feels the same way."

"Probably. I think she's worried about Mike being put

off that she doesn't have a lot of time for him, but it seems like he doesn't mind."

"She's making too much of it. I think she's still a little afraid to accept that things are going great for her in the romance department." Claire tapped Maxi's hand. "And I see things are going great for you and James too."

Maxi smiled. "They are. And you and Rob have settled into being amicable competitors."

Claire laughed. "I guess I was a little overly suspicious of him at first. But things are great now. In fact, things seem great with everyone. Life is nearly perfect."

"Yep." Maxi's gaze slid to the easel again. "Everything is *nearly* perfect."

CHAPTER THIRTY-SIX

*L*iz took one last tour around the house to make sure everything was perfect. She'd set out an array of appetizer trays on her parents' old dining room table. Nothing fancy. Just some cheese and crackers, ranch dip with carrots and celery slices, and basil and mozzarella crostini. The tomatoes and basil were straight from the garden. She'd spent hours there weeding, pulling up dead plants, and trimming. It was almost fall, so she'd harvested the last of the vegetables.

She'd made a watermelon mint punch, which sat in her mother's old crystal punch bowl on the kitchen table.

She'd even found some vintage paper plates and napkins with a party theme in the dining room hutch and had set them out.

It was a small party, but it felt like the first time entertaining in her new home. Except this wasn't her new home… not yet. Because her siblings had successfully avoided her calls. And now she would have to force them to talk to her before it went on the market.

Claire and Maxi were the first to arrive. Claire was carrying a large bakery box, and Maxi held a tray of brownies.

"You guys didn't need to bring anything. It's only a small gathering," Liz said as she ushered them in.

"Oh, these are just brownies from a mix, but Claire brought one of her masterpieces." Maxi pointed at the box. "Wait until you see it."

They unboxed it in the dining room. Liz couldn't believe the sight of the tall cake shaped like a sandcastle complete with turrets and ramparts. The cake even had sugar-encrusted frosting that made it look just like it was made of sand. "It's too pretty to cut into."

"Trust me, you'll want to cut it because it tastes just as delicious as it looks," Maxi said as Claire beamed with pride.

Jane and Andie arrived next with a tray of cookies. Bunny rushed over from her house to join them at the door with seven-layer dip and tortilla chips.

"You all didn't have to bring food. I have plenty. I'll have enough to feed the whole town!"

Jane had Cooper on a leash. "I wasn't sure if it was okay to bring him, but I know you pay a lot of attention to him at Tides."

"Of course it's okay. We had a dog growing up, actually." Liz pointed at the family picture on the mantel. She was delighted to have a dog in the house again. And if she was lucky enough to live here, maybe she could get her own... but she was getting ahead of herself. She saw no sense in getting her hopes up.

Sally, Emma, and Sheila arrived, and Liz gave everyone a tour of the small house.

"It looks fantastic," Bunny said. "You did a great job painting as usual, Sal."

"Thanks."

"And the house looks great without the clutter. You're pretty good at putting together the accents and moving things around." Maxi fluffed a pillow.

"So how come you don't want to stay here?" Sheila dipped a tortilla chip into the seven-layer dip and shoved it into her mouth.

Liz sighed. "I actually do want to stay. But it's complicated because I'm not the only one inheriting."

"Seems like there should be a way if you really want it." Bunny balanced a small plate with several appetizers in one hand and a glass of punch in the other.

"Yeah, you can't let your siblings rule. You have some say in this too. Have you talked to them?" Sally asked in her usual blunt manner.

"I tried to, but they've been putting me off."

"You shouldn't let them. You just tell them what you want. You might be surprised at their answer," Bunny said.

The doorbell rang, which was odd because everyone Liz had invited was already there. She hoped a neighbor wasn't coming to complain.

Liz opened the door, and her mouth dropped open in surprise.

"Lizzy!" Peter and Shelly stood in the doorway. They were both smiling ear to ear and wearing old clothes, as if they were ready to roll up their sleeves and get to work.

"Hi." Liz was at a loss for words. "I wasn't expecting you guys."

"We know. We wanted to surprise you," Shelly said.

"So you weren't brushing me off?"

"Of course not. We had this planned. We both feel so bad that you did all this work, and we want to help. We arranged to come here and wanted it to be a surprise. We were afraid we'd blurt it out. That's why we acted so weird on the phone." Shelly looked into the house over Liz's shoulder. "Are you having a party?"

Liz got over her shock and opened the door wider. "Yes, please come in."

Feelings of family warmth bubbled up as Liz introduced her brother and sister around the room. They hadn't been ignoring her. They'd been making plans to come and help!

Peter and Shelly seemed shocked at the changes.

"This looks so nice. I haven't been here in ages, but I remember it looking all cluttered and old." Shelly turned slowly and took in the living room. "Wow, so many childhood memories here."

Sally stood on the side, arms crossed over her chest. "Liz made this really homey, and she's really taking a liking to the town again."

Bunny stepped over beside Sally. "Your dad would love the way it's come out. He always said this home was a part of the family."

Sheila piped in from the other side of the room. "And it would be a shame to sell this little gem to some stranger."

Shelly frowned. Then her eyes widened, and she looked at Liz. "Wait, you mean you would want to live here?"

"Oddly enough, I think I do. It has all happy memories of our childhoods, and I'm looking for a new place. But I know you guys want your share from the sale—"

"Well, not right away," Peter interrupted. "I know this isn't a giant estate or anything, but Dad always said he wanted to keep it in the family. We all have our own homes now out of town, so I never thought to broach the subject with you guys."

"He said that?" Her father had never said that to Liz, but then again, she hadn't spent much time with him in the last few decades, and the last several years after the stroke made it harder and harder for him to talk.

"Yep. I didn't know that you had no place to go, though. I thought you were thinking about buying the place you were living in?"

Liz had told her siblings that so they wouldn't worry. "Unfortunately, that didn't work out. And now that I've been back in town, I've decided I really like it here. I need a fresh start."

"Then I say you have it here. We can work things out.

Can't we, Peter?" Shelly turned to their brother, who nodded.

"I think that sounds like a good plan. Dad would love it." Peter opened his arms, and the three hugged, just like they had when they were little kids.

"But you have to promise we can come and visit," Shelly said as they released each other.

"Of course." Liz would love to spend more time with her siblings.

"We'll just call Dad's lawyer and see what we can work out. Maybe a rent-to-own sort of situation?" Peter said.

"That sounds perfect," Shelly agreed. "You can pay us bit by bit, whenever you have extra."

"Great. Let's eat. I'm starving." Peter headed toward the dining room.

They cut Claire's sandcastle cake, and everyone took a piece.

"This is delicious," Bunny said to Maxi. "I'm glad Liz is staying. She's going to be a good neighbor. And Claire can bring cake any time."

Maxi laughed. "We'll be sure to drop by often."

Bunny's expression turned serious as she scraped some frosting onto her fork. "How is the painting going?"

"I think I'm getting there. Your lessons really helped." Maxi was happy with the progress she'd made, but she still felt a niggle of uncertainty. "But enough about me. What about you, Liz? How does it feel now that you are going to stay?"

Liz looked like she was still processing the information. "It's exciting. But also scary. I mean, it's very generous of my brother and sister to be so flexible with the payments, but I still need to pay them something, and there will be utility bills and other expenses. I have some savings, but I'm going to need to get a job."

Andie, who was cutting herself another piece of cake, looked over. "You do?"

"Yeah, well, maybe not full-time but at least part-time. I took early retirement from teaching when I thought my husband and I were going to travel together." Liz made a face.

"Sounds like he wasn't very nice," Bunny clucked soothingly. "I bet you can find something around here. Though it might be hard now at the end of the season."

"I have the perfect thing!" Andie turned to Jane. "Liz was brilliant at chatting up the guests at Tides. She'd be perfect for the position."

"Position?" Liz asked.

"We need someone part-time at the inn," Andie said, glancing at Jane. "Unless you found someone?"

"I haven't." Jane smiled. "Liz would be brilliant. The job is yours if you want it."

"Oh." Liz looked stunned. "Well, I certainly do like talking to people. And it seems like fun work. We'd need to work out hours and salary, but I'm definitely interested."

Jane looked overjoyed.

"Well, this is nice. Seems like things are working out

for everyone." Sally sipped a glass of punch. "What about your Civil War guy, Andie?"

All eyes turned to Andie, and her cheeks heated. "I sort of gave up on that."

"Gave up?" Sally's incredulous expression indicated she'd never given up on anything in her life.

"What's this about a Civil War guy?" Sheila asked.

Andie told the other party guests about her quest. "I've looked through all the archives, been to the town hall, even the Civil War museum in Arundel. I managed to trace his family through a few generations, but all mention of the Koslachowski family seems to just disappear in the early 1900s."

Bunny's fork clattered to her plate, and all eyes jerked in her direction. "Wait. Did you say Koslachowski?"

"Yes, the Civil War discharge papers were for Robert Koslachowski." Andie looked hopeful. "Do you know the family?"

"Know them? I am them. That was my family name."

"But I don't understand. I couldn't find any mention of it in recent times."

"That's because my grandfather had it changed." Bunny sighed and put her plate down on the table. "It was just too hard to pronounce, so he changed it to Koslo. That's my maiden name. It caused a rift in the family, actually. My uncle had a falling out with my father and grandfather over it. Then Gramps's house burned down, and we thought we'd lost everything. Where did you say this box came from?"

"It was found in the attic of a house that was foreclosed on. The house was on Maple Street."

"I don't know if any of my relatives owned a house there. The two families haven't spoken since the rift between my father and his brother. I don't even know my cousins." Bunny's expression turned hopeful too. "Was there anything else in the house?"

"There was some china and silver."

"That might have been from my family." Bunny was downright excited now. "I thought it was all lost in the fire, but I guess my uncle must have had some family things all these years."

"I can keep the items set aside for you," Andie offered. "None of it has been sold yet, since I just got it in."

"I would be so grateful if you did that. Truth be told, I was getting a little envious of Liz having all these wonderful family heirlooms around." Bunny gestured at several items around the room.

"Hopefully now you can have some of your own," Andie said.

"Wow, that worked out good," Emma said.

"Looks like you're moving to a great town with great neighbors, Sis." Shelly sounded almost envious.

"She sure is." Sally put her arm around Liz's shoulders. "Welcome to Lobster Bay. I think you're really going to like it here."

CHAPTER THIRTY-SEVEN

Two weeks later...

"Here's to new friends." Claire raised her coffee mug and clinked it with Liz then turned to Jane, Maxi, and Andie and added, "And old ones, too, of course."

They were seated on the outdoor patio at Sandcastles for one of their last outside morning get-togethers. The weather had turned chilly, and they were all bundled in sweaters. The patio heaters were running to help ward off the cold. The only other people braving the chill this morning were a pair of older women who sat at a table in the corner.

Liz had moved into her family home and started working at Tides right away. No new guests had checked in, but Jane had kept busy teaching Liz the ropes. Jane had invited Liz to their coffee chat and left Brenda in charge—not that there was much to do with no guests in residence.

Jane, Claire, and Maxi had been meeting for years like this. They'd recently added Andie to the mix when she'd moved to town, and now they had Liz. If things kept up this way, Claire was going to have to get bigger tables.

"Did Shelley and Peter get home okay?" Andie asked.

Shelley and Peter had stayed for almost two weeks helping Liz spruce up the house. Jane could tell Liz loved reconnecting with them, but adult siblings could only stay under the same roof for so long, and she sensed that Liz was happy for them to go home.

"They did. Shelly flew out yesterday and Peter the day before." Liz bent down and petted Cooper. "I'm going to miss them. It's a little lonely in the house now all by myself."

"I'm sure Bunny is happy to drop over quite frequently," Maxi joked.

Liz laughed. "She is a character, but truth be told, the camaraderie in that neighborhood is one of the things that sold me on staying."

"There's nothing like having great neighbors," Jane agreed.

"Bunny really appreciated all those items you gave her," Liz said to Andie. "But she feels guilty taking them for free. She said she wanted to pay for them."

Andie waved her hand dismissively. Jane could tell she was embarrassed. Knowing Andie, she'd paid a fair price for the items, but Jane had learned that her sister had a sentimental side. She'd seen her giving items away to people who had a connection to them before.

"I was happy to get those Civil War papers to the rightful owner. I put a lot of work into that. I didn't pay very much for the whole lot, and I just couldn't find my way to charging her."

Liz switched her attention to Cooper again. Maxi watched her thoughtfully as she petted and talked to the dog.

"You know, there are some nice dogs down at the Lobster Bay animal shelter just waiting for a good home," Maxi said.

Liz glanced up at her. "There's an animal shelter in town? Where is that?"

"Over next to the real estate office on Main Street."

Liz stopped petting Cooper and grabbed her coffee mug. "Thanks for letting me know. I might pay them a visit. Now that I have my own place and no one to tell me what to do, there's nothing stopping me from getting a dog."

"Speaking of dogs…" Jane nodded toward the door through which Bert and Harry were exiting the bakery and stepping onto the outdoor patio.

Maxi squirmed in her seat and glanced down at the large shopping bag sitting next to her chair. She'd refused to tell anyone what was in it, but now that Jane saw how nervous she was getting at the sight of Bert and Harry, she had a pretty good idea of what was in there.

"Oh look!" Andie leapt out of her chair and rushed to Bert and Harry. Jane leaned to the right to see around Claire, who was blocking her view. Bert and Harry were smiling from ear to ear as they looked down at their new addition, a little dog that looked like a terrier mix.

"You got another dog. That's wonderful!" Jane rushed over and petted the dog, who basked in the attention. Cooper trotted over, a little more cautiously than Jane and Andie. Everyone stood back and let the two dogs sniff each other. At first, they went slowly, touching their noses then down their bodies. Then the little dog adopted a playful stance, and Cooper wagged his tail. It looked like they would become good friends.

"No one can ever replace Goblin, but little Chloe here has already started to heal our hearts," Bert said.

Maxi cleared her throat, and everyone looked her way. She stood, the big shopping bag in her hand. As she reached into it, Jane could see the anxiety on her face.

"Maybe this will help you heal even further." Maxi pulled out a canvas with the most realistic pet painting Jane had ever seen. She half expected the likeness of Goblin to wag its tail or let out one of Goblin's soft woofs.

Bert and Harry's expressions morphed from surprise to delight with just a tinge of sorrow. They clearly loved it. Bert reached out for the painting then clutched it to his chest. "Oh, Maxi, it's perfect. Thank you so much."

He held it out again so everyone could see. "It looks just like her. Even has that little glint in her eye that she would get before she got into zoomie mode, don't you think?" Bert asked Harry.

Harry smiled. "It sure does. And look how she

captured the coloring and that little white spot above her nose just perfectly."

They both rushed over and hugged Maxi. "Maxi, we can't thank you enough."

Maxi beamed with pride. "I was happy to do it. In fact, I have a couple of other surprises in here." She reached into the bag and pulled out two small canvases. One was a painting of Cooper that she presented to Jane, and the other was a painting of Urchin that she gave to Claire.

"Thanks so much." Jane was truly touched by the gift. She held the painting next to Cooper so everyone could see how much it looked like him. "Mike will love this."

"I love it," Claire said as she admired the painting of Urchin.

"I was happy to stretch my artistic wings and do something different," Maxi said.

They chatted with Bert and Harry for a few more minutes until Chloe pulled them away, leaving the girls alone out on the patio.

"Was that one of the dogs you saw down at the animal shelter?" Liz asked Maxi.

"Yes, but there are a few others. Don't worry."

Liz laughed. "Sounds like I better get there quick if I want to have my pick."

"So many people are getting dogs that I think I better set up a dog watering station here on the patio," Claire said. "Maybe some water bowls and a faucet. I could even branch out into baking dog treats."

"That's a good idea, but I think outdoor season is almost over for this year. Maybe there are a few more mornings for the diehards, and then we'll have to move it inside for the cold weather." Jane bit into her chocolate chip muffin and made yum-yum noises.

"It was really nice of you guys to invite me today," Liz said. "Hopefully I'll be checking in guests at Tides next time, though."

"We do have one guest coming in a few weeks. It's kind of odd because this is really the dead season, and he was a little mysterious," Jane said.

"Mysterious how?" Liz asked.

Jane shrugged. "I don't know. He just seemed a little hesitant about giving his name and information."

"Is he an older gentleman? I find that older people are hesitant to give that information over the phone. Don't worry. I'll make sure he feels right at home," Liz said.

"If anyone can, it's you."

"Thanks. I meant to mention that Bunny had an idea that might bring more people to Tides in the off-season."

"I'm all ears," Jane said. "What is it?"

"A book club."

"Would that bring guests to Tides? Sounds like Bunny just wants to have some get-togethers," Maxi joked.

"That's probably true. The book club itself wouldn't bring in new guests, but she did have a good idea about coupling it with book signings. You could make an event out of the book signing, and then it would at least elevate awareness for the inn." Liz picked a cheese danish from the tray. "People might not stay overnight for the book signing, but they'd get to see the inn and might come back on their summer vacations to stay."

"That's not a bad idea. I always wanted to make a library in that back room next to the kitchen." Jane turned to Andie. "Remember Dad wanted to do that? But then we have to build bookshelves and get books. It was a lot of work, and he never got around to it. But that room would be a great one to have the book club in. It's got a fireplace and all those windows looking at the ocean."

"I think it's a great idea. I love reading," said Andie.

"We could invite Bunny and Sally and that nice Emma that we met at your party, Liz," Jane said.

Liz eyed Cooper. "And I suppose dogs will be allowed, right?"

Jane laughed. "Of course. Dogs are always allowed at Tides."

"Sounds like a plan, but there's one detail we have to nail down," Claire said.

"What's that?" Jane asked.

"What book are we going to read first?"

****

The bookclub turns out to be a lot more interesting than anyone anticipated!

A mysterious guest at Tides has piqued Bunny's suspicions but when she tries to find out what the guest is up to, she ends up on the radar of a retired detective who thinks Bunny is the suspicious one.

Meanwhile, Mike is planning a surprise for Jane…. But it's not what you think. Claire starts a new venture, only to find that the one person in town she wants to avoid is her biggest competitor.

How does it all end? Preorder Seaside Bookclub and find out!

Join my newsletter for sneak peeks of my latest books and release day notifications:
https://lobsterbay1.gr8.com

ALSO BY MEREDITH SUMMERS

Lobster Bay Series:

Saving Sandcastles (Book 1)

Changing Tides (Book 2)

Making Waves (Book 3)

Shifting Sands (Book 4)

Seaside Bonds (Book 5)

Shell Cove Series:

Beachcomber Motel (Book 1)

Starfish Cottage (Book 2)

Saltwater Sweets (Book 3)

Pinecone Falls Holiday Series:

Christmas at Cozy Holly Inn (Book 1)

Meredith Summers / Annie Dobbs

Firefly Inn Series:

Another Chance (Book 1)

Another Wish (Book 2)

ABOUT THE AUTHOR

Meredith Summers writes cozy mysteries as USA Today Bestselling author Leighann Dobbs and crime fiction as L. A. Dobbs.

She spent her childhood summers in Ogunquit Maine and never forgot the soft soothing feeling of the beach. She hopes to share that feeling with you through her books which are all light, feel-good reads.

Join her newsletter for sneak peeks of the latest books and release day notifications:

https://lobsterbay1.gr8.com

This is a work of fiction.

None of it is real. All names, places, and events are products of the author's imagination. Any resemblance to real names, places, or events are purely coincidental, and should not be construed as being real.

SEASIDE BONDS

Copyright © 2022

Meredith Summers

http://www.meredithsummers.com

All Rights Reserved.

No part of this work may be used or reproduced in any manner, except as allowable under "fair use," without the express written permission of the author.

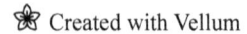

❦ Created with Vellum